TWICE MARKED

THE ALPHA AND HIS WITCH

DEADLY SECRETS STORY

BOOK 2

E. BOWSER

CONTENTS

I dedicate this book to my family. Thank you for your love and for supporting me in what I love to do.

Please subscribe to my website for updates on all series and what is coming up next! Also, we authors love reviews, so please leave one if you can!

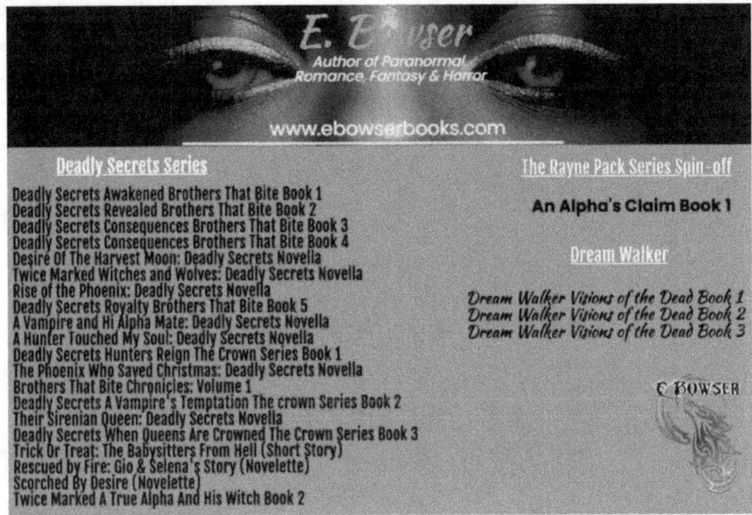

~ E. Bowser

www.ebowserbooks.com

ACKNOWLEDGMENTS

I want to thank God for letting me be able to write the stories that I love. I also want to thank my mother and the love of my life for putting up with me. I want to thank my friends that keep pushing me and believing in me. Big thank you to Sinful Secrets with a Deadly Bite Group, who always has my back whenever I release. All of you have supported me through this series. Thank you to everyone who read the series that contacted me on Facebook, Twitter, IG, and TikTok. I always love to hear from you, and please leave a review if you can. That is what keeps me writing.

CHAPTER 1
LATOYA

Even though my mother was gone, I still couldn't help but smile at my bestie finally letting Michael lock it down. I never understood why she didn't want the big wedding because I knew for sure that I would have one, and I did. I wanted all the over-the-top things for my wedding, but I understand what's more important now. As I watched them both greet the bougie Vampires, Government officials, and more of the one percent crowd, I understood why she didn't give two shits about having a wedding. It was all a show for these people, but it was a tradition for the Vampires. I knew why she did it when I looked at Michael's face. He didn't want this either, but he knew what it meant for their people. Shid, their people. Just saying that makes me realize we are living in a different and bigger world now. What we have with our men ran deeper than a piece of paper or words. We had something so much more, and nothing could break it. Not even being dragged to Hell would damage our bonds with them.

"Mama!" I looked down at Reign in my lap as she smiled at me with a slight red glow in her eyes.

"No shifting Reign. We will not have another Halloween show at your aunt's wedding, and you will not mess up your pretty dress mommy had made for you," I said as I kissed her cheek. Reign's smile fell, but two massive hands came into view before the waterworks started. I knew who it was in an instant because I could smell the asshole nature of him.

"Aww, what's wrong with the little puppy? Come give Uncle D some love."

"Give me my child, you ass—"

"Unc D! Unc D!" Reign giggled as she gave him slobber kisses on his face. I watched as his face screwed up, and I felt delighted by his reaction.

"Good job, Reign. Give him some more," I smirked. He glared at me, but I gave him the finger where Reign couldn't see.

"Let's go Reign and sit at the adult table instead of this little kiddy table made for people who have no knees. Now can you say... vertically challenged..." I stood up quickly and opened my mouth to cuss his ass out, but I felt arms around my waist, and a sense of peace settled around me. I reached back as Quinn pulled me away from Damon's punk ass and into a slow dance as the music played. I could hear Reign giggling and babbling non-stop as they moved through the crowd.

"I'm going to burn his ass alive one of these days," I said.

"He is an asshole, but he's actually not all that bad," Quinn laughed. I twisted out of his arms to stare up at him with my hands on my hips.

"What! You got to be kidding. He got Riaan to set my damn shoes on fire! On fire, Quinn. My perfect shoe collection was destroyed. He is the biggest asshole of assholes..." I leaned in a bit closer. "And a psycho serial killer," I said that last part in a whisper because I knew the Government types were trying to get information. I had already destroyed listening devices, mini cameras, and anything else these slick bitches had with them, but I was still careful.

Quinn almost choked on his laugh, but he pulled it together when he felt the heat coming off me.

"Okay, okay, LaToya. Chill the hell out. He did replace all your shoes and helped teach the twins how to control their powers, but this is Taria's day, so let's table it for now. First of all, you know deep down he isn't what we thought, regardless of the shoes," Quinn smiled. His hands found my hips as he pulled me closer to him. I couldn't wrap my mind around Damon's truth of what he had to do for his family. I just couldn't unsee him draining Taria until she died.

"Yeah, okay. It is buried so deep down I can't seem to find it. He's crazy as fuck," I said. Shaking my head.

"But...you really don't fight it when he holds our children. You may talk shit to him, but babe, you just let Reign go with the so-called Psycho," Quinn said. He spun us around, and I saw the Demon holding my baby girl. He looked at her, nodding along with whatever nonsense she babbled at him, and he just...listened patiently. It was weird as hell, and I was not jumping on the team Damon train. Fuck that! But he is good with the kids, which is crazy. I felt like my brain was about to explode because I trusted his crazy ass somewhere way deep.

"I'm not worried about our children. They can whip his ass as needed," I said. Quinn stopped us and stood utterly still as if something was happening. "Wha.." I never finished the statement when I heard Michael shouting at people to move. Quinn's nostrils flared at that moment, and the red ring in his eyes blazed brighter.

"LaToya, Taria is in labor!"

"Oh shit! It's too early," I cried. Not another second was wasted as Quinn grabbed me by the waist, leaped over tables of people, and landed beside Michael matching his pace as if we just walked up to him.

"Toya! Why didn't you tell me about the pain?" Taria screamed. I assumed her Vampire ways would make it easy.

"Oh, damn. My bad," I winced. Taria stared at me as her eyes flashed with lightning, and I heard the rumbling of thunder off in the distance. Then the chick just growled at me.

~

Deadly Secrets

I SAW the irritation on Michael's face, and I guess everyone else saw it as well because they all started to move.

"I am about to say fuck it and teleport us to the clinic," Michael gritted.

"No! Keep this pace. I don't know how that will affect her or the baby right now..." I felt a breeze at my side and heard my baby giggling. I turned to my left, and Damon was with us, and he handed Reign over to me.

"The baby is afraid...but I can't tell about what," He said. I looked up at him, and I knew my eyes were wide, and he looked back at me. Quinn had a hand resting on Taria's belly as Michael supported her to help her walk.

"Agreed," Quinn said quietly. We were outside now, quickly moving toward the clinic where everything had been set up according to Marcus and Camron's instructions. I looked at Quinn and back at Damon.

"We will not let anything happen, Toya," Damon said. I felt his hand rub my shoulder, and I calmed slightly. Just him being nice was weird as fuck, but I needed it.

"Quinn, what the hell is happening? She is a Vampire, and we know how long those can take. Not to mention we know our daughter is a dragon, and they do deliver faster than a Vampire but not this damn fast. What is happening?" Michael said as the doors ahead of us opened by the force of his thoughts. I knew it was him because the doors were outlined in a golden light. "I can't see what the fuck is happening!" Michael growled, making the ground shake slightly beneath us. Everyone was noticing us moving quickly away. Suddenly, I saw Camila and Malia seemingly slip out of the shadows and begin moving from guest to guest, trying to calm the masses while keeping the idiots out of our business. I could see a few officials pointing in our direction and some of the Blue Bloods watching with narrowed eyes.

"I'm not sure, but I need to check her out. Marcus and Cam should already be there waiting," Quinn said. His veins glowed blue as he used his gift as a healer to lessen her pain.

"Can y'all stop talking about me like I am not here?" A flash of lightning lit the sky.

"You good, sweetheart. We are just trying—"

"If y'all don't get this little girl out of me soon, the coming storm will turn into a damn hurricane!"

I wasn't about to say anything because she wasn't about to give me that death stare like she was giving Michael. Then she burst into tears as we hit the corner. I saw Cam standing in the doorway at the end of the hall, looking hella good, but worried. His usual playful manner was not present as he watched Quinn and Michael help Taria into the room. Reign was quiet while she lay on my shoulder with her fingers in her mouth. I bounced her as they got Taria onto a massive bed that looked as if it could fit twenty people on it at once. I saw a shadow move from the corner of my eyes as Blossom stepped out with swirling, colorful eyes. She looked as if she was about to fuck someone up until she realized it was the baby causing all of her Queen's pain. She looked at me as if I could tell her what to do. I did not know how to command no Shade, nor did I want that job.

"This is how it goes, Blossom. It will all be okay. Taria is fine," I said. Reign raised her head from my shoulder and smiled at the Shade. I had no hesitation and handed my baby off to the Demon, which is crazy as hell, but what isn't nowadays?

"She's fine? Fine! You think this is fine, LaToya! What in your mind would think any of this is fine?" Taria screamed. My eyes went wide, and everyone just looked around. Damon stepped forward, and I waited for his ass to get it.

"Lil sis, Toya is just saying that you got this, that's it," he said, kissing the top of her head. My mouth fell the fuck open as Taria deflated. Even Michael looked affronted as Taria patted Damon's hand like he was just so damn sweet. Damon turned to face me with this evil-ass grin on his lips.

"Sorry, I'm sorry. I don't know why I am acting like this at all. It's like I have four personalities in my head screaming at me. I'm sorry, Toya, Damon is right; I know he is," she cried. I pointed at Damon, and nobody saw the black eyes and evil as fuck smile he had on his face, except for me.

"Nobody sees this shit?"

"Shit! Shit!" Reign giggled as she played with Blossom's braids. I slammed my mouth shut because I forgot my baby was in the room. Quinn looked up at me with a frown, and I just threw my hands up. I heard a slight chuckle, making me look back at Damon as he rubbed Taria's head. He grinned at me with eyes almost as light as Michael's. Ain't no way that boy's middle name is Angel. Ain't no fucking way! Michael knelt beside Taria, and Marcus and Camron moved around the room, setting things up. It looked nothing like a typical hospital room, and there were no monitors or machines at all. I felt a brush of some kind of magic that flowed along with my senses, making me turn back to Damon. His hand glowed a faint golden color each time he contacted Taria's head. I knew this bastard was up to something! I stepped forward when the doors busted open, and Katherine, Selena, and Kya came inside.

"Damon is..."

"Oh good, Damon. Good idea in keeping the baby calm. That will lessen any pain or anxiety Taria feels," Katherine said. She looked at me, smiling with a light in her eyes I hadn't seen since we rescued her from the Van Allan family. I closed my mouth again. That shit was hard as fuck. I wasn't about to mention the scorch marks on the bottom of her dress either. Katherine smirked and raised both brows at me.

"Yes, yes, good job, Demo...ahh Damon," I smiled. I looked at Kya, who was talking with Marcus and Cam, before turning around to catch Blossom showing Reign fireballs.

"Okay, you two cut that out for now," I said, shaking my head. Kya came over, practically bouncing on her toes.

"I am so excited. This has been written about in many, many scrolls. The firstborn dragon! I can't wait!" Kya squealed.

"Oh wow, that is crazy as hell. Selena is a dragon, though, and I know there were more or are more of them somewhere," I said. Selena stood by Taria with a frown on her face before looking up at us.

"Kya is somewhat correct. There hasn't been a born Dragon of The Royal House Daemon ever, and I am sure that is what the true translation says," Selena said with a smile. My eyes were wide because how much more Royal could a family be at this point? I heard Kya gasp, making me turn toward her, seeing that her nose was buried deep inside a book that appeared out of nowhere. Where in the hell did that huge thing come from? Cause she didn't have it a second ago.

"She's right! I mistranslated. There is another passage written along the side about a Royal Family and the birth of..."

"Of what? The dragon baby?" I asked.

"I don't know. It...it just cuts off right there. Almost as if the next page was removed or never written," Kya said.

"It has been more than likely destroyed. Some things cannot be foretold, or they will change things. At least, that is what we were told long ago, and I guess Ashriel thinks this is one of those times. No matter, we know what this child is. But, I do not know why Taria is having so much trouble," Selena said. I looked at my best friend, and before I knew it, I was standing beside Michael and knocking Damon aside.

"Got damn Angels. Always into some shit," I muttered.

"Hey! Watch your micro-steps," he growled. I leaned over Taria, completely ignoring him, and kissed her forehead as I whispered. Apparently, my growing powers leaned more on the death side, but I couldn't ignore my other gifts. Those passed on to me from my mother. Rhonda was a healer first and foremost, so the words I whispered seemed to calm her enough to let her eyes fall shut. I stood back up and stepped back and deliberately onto Damon's foot.

"Oh, my bad," I smiled. Then just thinking about his name had me snapping my head to Katherine. "Kat, please do not tell me you named this fool after Selena's Royal house name," I muttered.

"Kat! Since when have you let anyone call you...call you Kat," Damon said before turning his glare on me.

"Yes, LaToya, I did," she laughed.

"That is right. My greatness doesn't end with just my name, though, Witch," he smiled. I rolled my eyes at his dumb ass.

"I can even teach you all about how to use that little Death magic you've been hiding."

My head snapped to him, and I stared at him for what felt like hours. Everyone moved around us and seemed not to pay us any attention, which was crazy. How in the hell was he in my mind? Taria, Quinn, and even Michael taught me how to shield my thoughts from everyone. He shouldn't...

"It's because we have many things in common. Such as the fight to stay on the right side of things. You can take the man out of Hell, but you can't take Hell out of the man. You were there, and you felt

it, Toya. You felt the increase in magic and the call. If you just feed it enough souls, you can access more."

I could feel my body shaking, and it was as if no one noticed, not even Quinn, that this Vampire, more like Demon, knew something I hadn't spoken a word of to anyone. His gaze burned a deep gold, and I couldn't move no matter how much I fought it until he looked away.

"Bastard," I gritted. He didn't look at me again, but I saw that damn grin I would slap off his handsome face. He should not even look how he does, but that's a Demon for you, always deceiving and shit. Michael stood up and looked out of the windows at the storm fast approaching. Taria began moaning before she started yelling. It looked like everything was directed at Michael, and I was glad it wasn't directed toward me. Michael looked back at her and moved to her side before catching Marcus's eyes. I frowned, trying to figure out what was up, but Michael pulled out his phone.

"Hello, hold on," Michael said as Taria cussed his ass out. It was like it didn't even phase his ass because even though she screamed, his hand rested on her forehead. "Marcus, is the baby coming or what?"

"Not yet, but," Marcus started.

"Cool. Taria," Michael said softly. He looked at her for just a second with the same look he gave her when he knocked her out during training.

"What!" Taria snapped. The lightning struck right outside of the window, and we all took a step away from the two.

"Sleep!" Everyone and everything was quiet except for a beeping noise that seemed to come from Kya before she dug inside her pocket to turn it off.

"Oh shit," I whispered before closing my mouth when Michael's gold eyes landed on me. I was not about to play with his ass right now.

"She is still screaming in my head right now, but something is off. I don't know what it is," Michael said. He looked at his mother before looking back at Quinn.

"Whatever happens, we got it, but she has to keep calm. I don't understand why she is up and down. Everything that I know and read shouldn't be happening like this. Right, Katherine?"

"Quinn is right. I don't know if it's because of everything that has happened or visiting Hell has changed things," Katherine stated. She looked at Selena, and she shook her head as well.

"I had no outbursts when I delivered Micah," Selena said. Michael looked at the closed doors and frowned as if he sensed something, but no one appeared.

"Everyone, we need all of you to get back. It's time," Marcus growled. His hands were placed in a bowl of water that glowed white as Camron stepped forward and raised one hand, letting it hover over Taria's belly. We all stepped away except Michael when Taria's eyes popped open, and she screamed.

The scream that ripped through the air didn't compare to the sound of the storm outside. Michael stood up as Marcus and Camron moved in and placed hands over Taria's belly. Quinn moved closer now with the sleeves of his dress shirt rolled up to his elbows. I stepped back along with everyone else. I moved closer to my mother, seeing that she looked as if she were ready to cry.

"Mother, this will all work out," I whispered. Just standing next to my mother again gave me a certain peace I hadn't been able to feel in such a long time. I knew there were still things I didn't talk with her about and things that I needed to work out on my own, but how do you bring up the day you destroyed your family?

"Yes, yes, I am sure it will. It's, it's just...it is the exact day you were born, Damon. Everything, everything that is happening feels as if history is repeating itself and..." She trailed off as she looked at me. We looked the same age, but her eyes told the truth of age. The weight of her age pressed down on me, but its brightness warmed my entire soul. I moved away slightly because I didn't deserve to feel the warmth of her light. My father's death was my fault, no matter why it happened.

"Do not worry. I do not believe that things will repeat themselves, mother. Taria's child will never have to do the things I have done," I stated. I needed to leave and get away for a while. I shouldn't be here in this moment, witnessing something so pure when I was so...

"That isn't what I mean, Damon. The skies cried this day over three hundred and seventy years ago. Well, three hundred and seventy-one years ago, to be exact. The day you were born was one of the greatest days in my life, and I would never change that," she said quietly. I didn't realize my hands were balled into fists until my mother's long, smooth fingers wrapped around mine. This was something we had always done with each other. Take a step into our own space, and it just be us.

"How could you still say that after all the shit I have done to this family?"

"You mean after all the shit you have done for this family? I know I can't make you see what I see in you, but I will be damned if I let you think that we don't understand the choice that was made. Your father would be proud of what you had to do to save your family, even if that meant he had to die because of it," she growled. Katherine wasn't like any other Vampire, just like I wasn't or Michael. We...we were something different.

"The baby is coming!" Quinn grunted. We both looked up simultaneously, breaking the moment as all sound crashed around us once more. I felt something beside me, and I looked down to see Toya squinting up at me.

"What the hell is wrong with you, tiny Tim?"

"I am on to you, Demon. You are up to something, and if you think that little Jedi mind trick you pulled will throw me off, you are completely fucked up in the head," she sniffed.

"Taria, I need you to push!" Quinn shouted. We all heard

and saw the lightning strike outside as Taria screamed. My mother was right about one thing today is precisely what it sounded like when I was born. I would rather forget some memories, but I had to keep that one. The look on my mother's face when she first held me told me what true love was, and that was another reason I hung on for so long.

"I don't know why this baby had to be born on your damn birthday. My Godchild was not supposed to come yet," she grumbled. I raised my brows because I wasn't expecting anyone to know what today was because it meant nothing and everything to me. "I had to plan that stupid ass after party for your unholy birthday just to be able to plan Taria's wedding. I still can't believe she got me to do that shit," Toya said, rolling her eyes.

I just stared at her until I felt tiny fingers pulling my hair, making me turn to see Blossom and Reign watching me.

"Unc D," she babbled. Reign looked at Taria and back at me with tears. "Make better, make better," she cried. Toya turned around and moved to take her baby when Taria cried out.

"Stop! Stop pushing," Quinn said. His face looked alarmed. I looked around and stopped the little Phoenix.

"Kya, please take Reign out of here," I said, looking at Toya. She was close to tears and no one knew what was happening. I knew she was distraught cause she did not even argue when Kya moved to do what I said.

"Quinn, what's the problem? What do you need?" I said, moving next to him.

"Damon, I need you to keep the baby calm. Marcus and Camron, I need you to keep healing, Taria," Quinn gritted. The power in the room was massive, and it felt as if weight or heavy pressure had filled the entire room.

"What do I need to do?" Michael said. I looked up at him, and for the first time, I could tell he was absolutely lost and out of the loop. He couldn't see what would happen, and I could tell he was trying to look. This was something he could never see, and I knew he had to know that.

"Mike, I need you right where you are," Quinn stated. Michael looked at our mother and grandmother and then at me. I nodded at him, telling him I wouldn't let shit happen to Taria or their baby without words. I didn't suffer through all this bullshit just for Taria to die now, and I would do whatever else was needed so they would make it through this in one piece. Taria screamed again as she gripped Michaels's hand. I could feel Toya moving around the room as she whispered, and then she eventually ended up next to Quinn. She placed her hand on his back and closed her eyes. I couldn't tell what she was saying, but I could feel the energy shift and the temperature drop dramatically.

"One more, Taria! One more!" Quinn yelled. Michael moved to help Taria lean forward just as she sucked in a breath and let out a growl that was more animalistic than human. Her light brown eyes flashed a brilliant ice blue before flashing to white. A small cry filled the now quiet room, and everyone looked at Quinn as he pulled another creature into the world. I removed my hands and looked at Taria, who fell back onto the pillows. Michael was beside her with his wrist in her mouth as Marcus and Cam kept a firm grip on her to make sure she healed.

"My God-baby! She is beautiful, Taria," Toya cried. Marcus looked up as Quinn and Toya cleaned the baby.

"Cam, you got this? I want to check on the baby," Marcus asked.

"Yeah, you good," Cam said with a frown.

"Is..is she.." Taria stuttered as she pulled her mouth from Michael's wrist. Michael never took his eyes off the baby. Toya brought the baby closer to Taria and placed the baby in Taria's arms. The little girl had her eyes closed until the door burst open. We all looked to the door as Garrett rushed through.

"I made it. Is...where..." Garrett shuddered as he ran over to Michael's side. "Hey, I'm here," he said, looking down at the baby. That little boy was just as creepy as his friend, but I got it. He could see spirits, so maybe he had been talking to this little one the entire time.

"Oh my God," Taria whispered. I looked back at the baby as she opened her eyes wider and stared into azure blue eyes rimmed with gold. This baby should not have been able to track as well as she was doing, but her eyes fastened on Garrett, and she smiled. "She shouldn't be able to smile yet, right? Right?" Taria said, looking around.

"What's her name, mom?" Garrett said as he pushed closer to Michael. I looked at my bother as he unconsciously pulled Garrett closer to him but couldn't take his eyes off his daughter.

"Genesis Icelyn Cross Vaughn," she smiled. The newest little Vaughn looked back at her mother, and they just stared at each other. I looked back toward the door, feeling something shift in the air, but I couldn't figure out what. I took a step and ended up standing in the doorway, sniffing the air.

"Taria! What's wrong? Quinn?" I turned back just as Toya reached out, taking the baby away as Taria screamed again. Every thought in my head faded away when she went limp.

"No! This is not supposed to happen! I did everything that was asked!" I growled. Michael looked at Quinn as he bit into his wrist and shoved it into Taria's mouth. Cam and Marcus both placed their hands on Taria as they began to glow.

"It's okay, Uncle Damon!" Garrett shouted, just as Quinn did the same.

"She is still in labor! She is having another baby!"

When I say everything went quiet, it was deadly silent.

"What the fuck did you just say?" Toya asked when a lightning strike hit directly outside the room once again. Michael moved his wrist just as Taria leaned in and screamed.

I looked toward my mother and grandmother, and both of their faces were in shock. Toya quickly moved to Selena and handed the baby over as she rushed back to Taria's side.

"Taria, it's all good. We will both have twins now. You got this!" Toya said, looking at Quinn. Quinn never took his eyes away from the new baby that was arriving, and I had no clue what was happening. This was not foretold. Ash said nothing about twins or another child! What the fuck was happening? My gaze landed on Garrett. He was standing beside Selena, but his eyes were glued to his mother. I started to take a step toward Taria because this...this was not supposed to be happening. What if going to Hell changed something? What if I fucked up and this child...this child wasn't a child at all?

"You were not told all, Damon, or have seen all. Your part in all this is not done. Those babies are the key, just like the Witch."

I felt my body freeze in place at Ashriel's voice in my mind. I wanted to scream and rip his damn wings apart. How would I protect anyone if I don't know what is to come? How would I protect anyone? What kind of fucked up game is this Angel playing?

"Push, Taria! Push! One more," Quinn grunted. I looked at Marcus and Cam and saw the strain on their faces as they controlled the pain we all could feel Taria experiencing. Another cry rang out in the room, but it wasn't from the baby that Quinn had just delivered.

"A boy! He's..." Quinn trailed off as he handed the baby to Toya, who quickly assisted him.

"A boy? He...he isn't crying! What's wrong? He...why isn't he..."

"Taria, he is fine. His eyes are open, and he is breathing. He's..."

"He what!" Michael shouted. I even saw the strain on his face as he helped Marcus and Camron hold Taria in the bed.

"Michael, he is fine! Chill the...I am just cleaning him up,"

Toya snapped. I couldn't move at the thought of me having to protect more of these creatures. Toya wrapped up the baby quickly and moved over to Taria and Michael. Taria seemed to push everyone away as she reached for her baby damn near, yanking him out of Toya's arms.

"Oh my...I..." Taria trailed off as she looked at her baby boy. I finally got my shit together and moved closer, seeing bright gold eyes staring at Taria as if he had stared at her all his life. His soul and gaze felt...it felt damn near ancient. Michael lightly touched the top of the baby's head.

"We...we have a son," Michael said. Taria stared at the baby, and I saw her eyes widen in shock or surprise before she snapped her head up.

"Naheem. His name is Naheem."

"Okay. I like that name, but we haven't even talked..."

"No, Michael. " Taria whispered, "he told me his name is Naheem, and Ra'ah is coming," Taria whispered. I heard my mother gasp just as Michael reached out to take his son.

"What the hell is happening?" Toya said when Taria screamed louder. This time no one said a word but moved as one when Taria started to bleed uncontrollably.

"Taria! Taria!" We all shouted as the earth began to shake.

Deadly Secrets

Someone or something was coming, and I had no clue what it could be. I can't stand all the cryptic messages I get from Ashriel. At least tell me what the fuck I need to do to help Taria. Both babies began to cry, and I moved over to them while maintaining my balance as the ground rolled and bucked beneath us.

"Damon, something is wrong! I feel it! My Queen she..." I

felt Blossom close to me, but my focus was on getting to the babies to calm them down. If anything, I knew Michael and Taria would not want them to be afraid, and God forbid they felt their mother's pain.

"Lend her your strength," I said. I looked into those swirling eyes and had no clue why I even said that shit. Taria is strong as shit, but something did not want these children to be born. There had to be another force at work, but I did not know who or what. Why was this such a secret that no one knew or could sense she had multiple children? I grabbed both children and held them to my chest, and I could feel their power. I could hear the tiny voice in my head that had me looking at Naheem in amazement. I could feel the little dragon growing cold in my arms and realized her crying was her way of getting upset. She protected the others, and now this other baby was in trouble.

"We need to get this baby out! Marcus! Something is blocking me...I can't pull out the baby!" Quinn said. Marcus pulled his hands away from Taria, and she let out a loud cry before she began to shake.

"What the fuck is happening?" Michael growled. I could tell he was trying and failing to see into the future, and nothing he did with all his power was helping the situation. I looked down at Garrett, but he was staring at the closed doors. That's when I felt the hairs on my neck stand on end as the doors burst open. My scent told me it was Femi, but my eyes narrowed in on the Druid beside him.

"Everyone out of the way, or she and that baby will die!"

Chapter 3
Latoya

I heard the words, but I was not about to move anywhere that wasn't next to my bestie. I didn't know who that tall ass chick was or is, but she was tripping. Apparently, Michael was thinking the same thing, but he knew something I didn't know. He moved and had the woman backed up against the wall with a hand around her throat.

"Why the fuck is there a Druid here, and what the fuck do you want?" He growled. I looked to Femi, but I did not remove my fingers from Taria's toes, and I felt like Blossom raised a brow in a challenge at the woman. She had appeared next to Taria in full-on shadow mode, but it was as if I amplified her feelings. I could feel the magical energy in the room, and I could tell Blossom was doing something to keep Taria tied to this earth. I had one hand on Quinn's back and the other touching Taria's leg. Marcus had moved to Quinn and began pushing healing energy, but nothing worked. Taria was bleeding out, and Quinn seemed to strain as he tried to pull the baby out of Taria.

"Michael! Let her go! She is here to help, not harm your children," Femi stated firmly. I had never seen a Druid female, not to mention one that didn't look fucked up.

"Femi, I don't know this Druid. I don't know one who would help without expecting something in return for more power," Michael growled.

"This baby is dying! We need to do something!" Cam growled. I looked up, and his eyes were damn near black. His fangs were long, and his hand shook, but the glow grew even more intense. I looked down at Taria, and her brown skin looked as if he were becoming gray.

"No! Hell no! Taria, you can't!" I screamed. I began chanting as I pushed my life force into her, feeling a breeze on my skin. I knew it was Michael. I heard something hit the floor, but I couldn't focus.

"I need everyone to step away if you want me to save them! Now!" The Druid shouted. I looked up, meeting Quinn's eyes, but he was staring at Michael.

"Listen to me, Michael. You may not trust this Druid, but I do! If you don't trust her, trust me!" Femi pleaded. "They are my blood, and I would never put them in harm's way."

It felt like it took Michael hours to reply, but I knew it was only seconds. None of us knew what the fuck to do, but if we did nothing, she would die. I was sure of it. I could see it written and the veil of death creeping closer. I knew that I could not keep death from coming if it were her time.

"Save them," Michael said as he raised his hands away from Taria. He made a motion with his hands that pushed every one of us away from the bed and Taria. We all hit the far wall, making me search for the babies, only to see Damon with a shield around himself, the babies, and Garrett. He wasn't even looking at Taria or this Druid, but he stared at Naheem as he cuddled Genisis close to his chest. The Druid seemed to float over to Taria as her hands glowed a deep red. I felt old magic, so old it made my bones ache. It was like what I felt when I called on that dark magic to reach my father but slightly different.

"To save a life, you must give up your own life. The one who gives wisdom must love life, for the one who believes in the higher power, let the living water flow through you. Whoever pursues righteousness and love finds life, and that is what I give to you."

It was as if all the energy and light were absorbed inside the room, making it grow warmer and warm before a sudden flash lit up the room. I blinked rapidly, trying to clear my vision to see what was happening. I never felt power like that before. It was life, death, and something else I couldn't figure out. I heard the whine of a baby and moved without my vision being clear. I blinked again, and things started to become clear. My legs hit the bed, and I felt my way around it, reaching out mentally to Taria, praying that I could still feel her in my head.

"She's beautiful, Toya."

I just about fell to my knees when I heard her voice in my head. I blinked again, and everything became clear. Michael was already next to them as Quinn checked Taria and the baby out. I made my way around the bed and stopped in front of the Druid. I looked up, and she turned her head toward me, and I realized how pretty she was, which was nothing like the Druids we all knew.

"Thank you," I whispered. She smiled tiredly as her champagne-colored eyes filled with tears.

"It was my pleasure and destiny to help this family," she replied. I reached out to hug her because I knew in my soul if she didn't come, Taria and my other God baby would have died.

"Thank you so much. You just don't know how much this means to me. What is your name?"

"Ahh, it's not a problem...ahh," she shuddered as she awkwardly hugged me back. "Saphreena, but you can call me Reena," Saphreena said. I couldn't place her accent, but that was normal around these parts.

"Cool. Thank you, Reena. Please let me know if you ever

need anything," I said, squeezing her hands. She smiled at me, and I turned to see Taria staring at me with all three babies in her arms. Marcus and Quinn were talking at the foot of the bed while Cam had both hands on Taria's stomach. I came up on Michael, and he moved slightly so I could get closer. With everything happening, there was no way we could leave tomorrow.

"You have outdone yourself, Taria. Three freaking babies, and you were talkin about me," I laughed. Michael was quiet, but he couldn't take his eyes away from the four people that made up part of his world.

"Believe me. I was not trying to outdo you. I have no clue what I will do with five kids," she laughed lightly.

"So, what's all of their names? Well, their full names?" I asked Taria. I looked at the triplets and gasped when I saw the troublemaker. Her eyes were slit like a cat, but the color looked like something you would see in the Alaskan sky at night. They were beautiful but felt as if they held power so old and deadly that I wasn't sure if we were meant to protect the kids or if they were born to protect us.

"I can tell you that Auntie Toya," Garrett said as he climbed onto the bed. While I spoke to Reena, I looked around and guessed that they had changed the bedding because this shit looked spotless. Where was this speed of clean up when I needed it back in the day?

"Oh, okay, Mr. Big Brother, what are their names?" I said, smiling. Garrett looked down at the babies, and they all stared back at him like he was teaching a class. I looked up, and Taria looked up at the same time. Her eyes were wide, and I knew exactly what she was thinking. These babies should not be this alert, but it shouldn't even be a surprise, especially when one of them can tell you their own name right from the jump! I shook my head. I know we would talk about all this shit another time.

"Well, first we have Genesis Icelyn Cross Vaughn. Dad and I chose her name together," Garrett said. Michael finally cracked a smile as he looked at his son.

"Yeah, we did, and I think we did a good job," Michael said as he placed a hand on little Genesis's head.

"Then we have Naheem Micah Cross Vaughn, right, mom?" Garrett said, looking at Taria.

"That is exactly what I was thinking, baby," she said. I looked at Michael, and I could have sworn he had a tear in his eye, but he looked away.

"Naheem Micah Cross Vaughn is a perfect name for my second son," Michael said, but he was looking at his mother while he spoke. I turned to Katherine, and Selena was next to her with her finger over her lips. Katherine had a tear rolling down her cheeks as she nodded. I couldn't help but smile because we barely have moments like this. It finally felt like we could get a break. We needed this, but my chest tightening told me it wouldn't last long.

"We all know my baby, baby, baby sister's name," Garrett smiled. "Ra'ah Zaria Cross Vaughn! Zaria is grandma Na'ki's middle name," Garrett stated, looking at Taria. Femi came closer to the bed. And looked at the babies, and I swear the youngest eyes flashed.

"Ra'ah Zaria Cross Vaughn. That name is more correct than you know, Taria," he said.

"Yes, and maybe you need to tell us how you knew what was happening and where did *"she"* come from?" Taria nodded toward Reena. She was right about that, but I couldn't care less since she saved her life.

"Saphreena has helped with births of power throughout our history. She was there when your mother was born. Our family has what you may call a bond with the Druids of the Amarachi lands. She is the last that hasn't turned to the darkness," Femi stated as he looked at all of us. "How about we thank Saphreena for now and speak to her later," Femi said. He moved to kiss Taria on her forehead when she nodded and congratulated Michael. I gave my baby Garrett a huge hug and told his little ass we would talk. He knew more of what was happening than any of us did.

"Okay, Auntie." Garrett laughed. He made his way out of the room, and I turned my attention back to the babies. Taria spoke with Reena for a quick minute, and the next thing I knew, it was just me, Taria, Michael, Quinn, Blossom, and the triplets left in the room. Michael sat in a chair next to Taria holding Genesis while Taria fed a greedy ass RaRa. Naheem was already fed and asleep, but RaRa was up like she didn't want to miss shit. I climbed onto the large bed and settled myself next to Taria while I waited for Quinn to finish up whatever the hell he was doing. He felt like he had to get all that happened typed up and saved for later review.

"So Auntie Toya, what do you think about your God BABIES," she said, shaking her head. She looked as if she couldn't believe it. Shit, I still couldn't believe it, and I watched the shit go down.

"I am excited. I will hold them all day, every day, and spoil the hell out of them like you did the twins," I laughed. Ra'ah finished up, and Taria positioned her to burp, but I held out my hands. "Gimmie, gimmie," I said. Taria chuckled and handed her over to me. I positioned her on my shoulder and patted her back lightly while Taria leaned into the pillows.

"You do know that you don't have time to spoil my babies right now, right?" I looked up at her, and I could tell she was drained. It took a lot for her to look tired physically, but she did now. The dark circles under her eyes told the truth in my thoughts, but I latched onto what the hell she just said.

"Why? I don't need to go anywhere anytime soon," I shrugged. I heard a little burp and smiled.

"Don't play dumb with me, Toya. It would be best to deal

with your people sooner rather than later. You can't put this off," Taria said. Michael shifted, and because he was so still, Taria and I both turned sharply to look at him. He stood up and placed his baby girl in the bassinet next to her brother.

"She is right, Toya. Something is up, and we all know it. Whatever was up with that Witch Valerie isn't going to stop at her. It's just going to keep happening," Michael said, looking at me. I looked down at Ra'ah as she yawned and stared back at me. Her eyes changed from green, red, pink, and orange. I smiled down at her, not trying to listen to these two because I didn't want to see the people who wanted to take me from my mother. The people who would have killed her if they could have found her years ago to take me. The very people who probably were down with that bitch that took my mother from me.

"Do you think they are right, RaRa?" I asked the baby. I jerked as her eyes flashed a bright green before she smirked at me. The energy coming from this girl was straight-up black air force energy. I looked at Taria and Michael, and he raised a brow. Taria's head snapped to the other babies, then looked at Michael. He looked into the bassinet and then back to Taria.

"What?" What's with the silent looks?" I snapped.

"Naheem says to tell you that the time is now," Taria stated slowly. I knew my face was saying what the fuck, but the door burst open before I could voice that.

"Why in the hell is your new creature calling my name repeatedly?" Damon growled. His eyes were gold as he looked from Michael to Taria and then to me as I would answer. I rolled my eyes and let out a long sigh.

"I don't know, but clearly, you are not needed here," I said.

"Yes. Yes, he is," Taria said, smiling. "Damon come in, close the door and just shut the hell up," Taria said.

"Listen, you might be Vampire Queen and all, but..."

"Damon! Close the damn door and bring your ass in here.

You are right, and she is Queen, and it seems you helped make that happen. So don't act like you don't respect the title," Michael said.

"Boy, if you don't go head with all that shit. I am not..."

"Aight, I will just ask our mother to..."

"Mannn... what? What do y'all want now? It's a limit to how long I can be around midgets," he chuckled.

"See, I didn't say anything, but Demon, I can bring that shit if you want it. You about on my last..."

Taria clapped her hands softly, but it caught our attention. I did manage to flick a finger sending heat his way.

"Damon, I will need you to do me a favor," Taria said. He patted his jeans as if they were on fire, and I smirked, happy for a second.

"What now?"

I heard Quinn close his laptop, so I looked over at him, seeing a look on his face I hadn't seen in a few weeks. Something was up with the wolves, and I knew we had to get this shit taken care of. I couldn't put off dealing with my family. I also couldn't put off dealing with the Witches and Warlocks, who still haven't bent the knee. I sighed, knowing Taria and Michael were right.

"I need you and Blossom to go with Quinn and Toya to handle business. I am not leaving the school for a while now to be on the safe side," she said. My head snapped around so fast I thought it would have fallen off.

"Taria! I know you fuckin lying!"

I looked at Taria and Michael like they had lost their damn minds. I knew childbirth was complicated, and they were most likely not thinking straight. There was absolutely no fucking way I was going anywhere with the tiny terror with heels. Naw, they had me fucked up!

"This would be the first and only time I will agree with the munchkin over there," I nodded toward Toya. She bared her teeth at me, but I shook my head.

"No one is joking, Damon. This is important, and I need to know my family is safe. I trust you and my Shade to watch over my best friend and her family. This is what I need from you," Taria said.

"We don't need nobody, especially a fool. Watching our backs? He just might stab me in the damn back!" Toya scoffed. I just smiled at her before turning my attention back to Taria.

I stared at her flashing fangs, but she didn't turn away, and Michael said nothing. He watched me and Taria stare each other down. Taria raised a brow while her light brown eyes glowed. This stare-down was something we started doing lately. It was as if we communicated silently to each other.

"Where the hell do we need to go? If I go, I need assurance

that SHE," I pointed at Toya, "grows at least four more inches," I said, turning around. I caught sight of Blossom, and her eyes swirled with every color I had ever seen. She licked her lips and smiled. What the hell was that? Was she flirting again, and why the hell were they teaching her shit like this?

"Thank you, brother," Taria said. Blossom said nothing, but it was almost as if I could feel her inside me. Before I could move, the doors burst open.

"Mommy! Mommy!" Lily screamed as Shani moved quickly to pick her up. Lily turned her bright-ass smile on me. "Hi, Uncle Damon. Are you here to see the babies?"

"I saw the baby's little princess. It's your turn now, but you have to whisper so you don't scare them," I grinned. We all knew Lily's whispers were actually the usual tone of voice. I had no fucking clue why I got all lovey-dovey when she was around. Lily was like a power puff girl with a double dose of chemical X.

"Oh, oh sorry," Lily laughed. Shani shook her head with a smile.

"Lily, when I put you down, walk slowly to mommy and daddy so you can see your little sisters and brother," Shani said as he put Lily on her feet. We watched Lily as she took giant slow steps to the bed, but Michael moved to pick her up in his arms, laughing.

"Come on, princess. You are a trip," Michael said as he took her to see the babies. Taria smiled, but she turned back to me.

"Stay for a minute now that Shani is here as well," Taria said as she looked over at Quinn. He was quiet and deep in thought before he looked up.

"Yeah, yes, Shani, stay here a moment. We all need to talk, but I know we all should get on the road soon. We need to speak with Dax and his Pack about Pack business while also getting LaToya's shit straight," Quinn said. Toya frowned like she expected him to veto me going. Shid, I was hoping he said hell naw, but it didn't happen. I flicked my eyes to the left when I felt Blossom next to me. Her voice was like music in my mind. It quieted the voices telling me I shouldn't be here and that no one would ever trust me.

"I know you can sense what my Queen is sensing. We need to do this, Damon. Or do you not think you can handle it? If so, I can do it myself. Our Queen needs us to protect what is important to her, and I know for a fact that is why you are here."

I didn't move or say a word. I could feel something growing out of control, and it was not that bitch Ida. Magic was thick in the air and throwing things off balance. I knew all this. Who did this Shade think she was, talking to me like that? It was as if she didn't know that I knew how to handle myself.

"You don't know anything, and I never said I wasn't going."

"If you didn't want to do it, you wouldn't even have told her about the darkness in her powers. I can feel that you are not just here because you finished your duty, but it's just the next phase of it."

"You don't know anything. Could you not read my mind, Shade? You may not like what you will see if you go deeper. My wrongdoings stretch far beyond what you may have seen in Hell."

"We shall see."

Blossom moved away and I felt as if a piece of me was missing. I wanted to explore what it was about her, but that isn't what I was here to accomplish. She was right about that, but I didn't even know the actual mission. The fact that I was still a pawn in this game called life was for the fucking birds. I looked at Taria and Michael, then the children, and put all my thoughts aside. I knew the reason why I was protecting them, but it didn't mean I had to like that shit. I turned around, crossed my arms, and stared at them. I looked at Toya, and she was standing shaking her head.

"Well, don't keep us all waiting since we have to leave soon. What is it exactly that we need to do? I hope it's killing something because I need to release this frustration," I grunted.

"Ha!" My head snapped to Toya as she laughed. I squinted at her little ass as she cried, laughing while pointing at me.

"What the hell is wrong with you?" I asked.

"You tryna release frustration on Blossom's ass, is what you want to do, by the way you eye it," Toya chuckled. I was not trying to deal with this shit, but this was just a glimpse into what I would be dealing with while we were gone.

"You stay fucking lying, bruh," I said. I watched that ass move, but there was no time for all that.

"Oh, I'm sorry. Toya showed me how to take pictures on this phone. If you like it, I can send you some pics of it so you can have it all the time," Blossom said with brows raised. I looked at Toya.

"That's why you don't need kids! The fuck are you teaching her?" I yelled, and all three babies started to cry.

~

Deadly Secrets

I STOOD there looking between Quinn and Toya. Shani was standing there in shock at the fact that she was going. I didn't know too much about the girl, but she wasn't as innocent as these four seemed to think. Shani was also more to the Pack than just another wolf or babysitter. I could tell things were serious, and as much shit as Toya talked, she was also worried. She may have a Circle, but it was all new to her, and she still needed to figure out who to trust. So, having to confront the other Witches who may have been involved with her mother's murder, she would need back up.

"And that is why you will go. They all need protection. You chose this path, Damon."

I hated that Ashriel could invade my thoughts anytime he felt it was necessary. It wasn't as if I wouldn't do it just because Taria asked me to do it. If anything happened to Toya, she would do whatever to get her back or avenge her friend. Doing all that may get her killed in the process. I witnessed that shit firsthand when I was the one who took her life. The shame and hate almost crushed me, but I pushed that shit back.

"So, we need to speak with the Rayne Pack and discuss the fact that children are going missing once again. Then go and handle Witches and Warlocks and make them bend the knee or break their knees," I said, looking at everyone.

"Yeah, that's about it and whatever else comes up in the process," Quinn said. He pulled out his phone and typed a quick text. "We should leave tonight," he said, frowning. Being the True Alpha was a hard-fucking job, and I would give it to the dog that he was handling it okay.

"What about the twins?" Taria asked. "They can stay with us..."

"No, no, they are coming with us. You need to take care of your five damn kids. Shani will be with us, so it will work out smoothly," Toya said. I watched as she kissed RaRa on the cheek before climbing off the bed and handing the little girl to Blossom.

"What? Are you sure? We have more than enough room and people to..."

"No, Taria. Take care of your babies and focus on yourself. We got this. Things will always come up or happen out of the blue. I...I just need to keep them close, you know?" She finished.

"I got you, bestie, but this is more reason for Damon and Blossom to go with you, so no more of the bullshit that you are talking. They will go, and that is that," Taria said pointedly. Toya started to argue, but Quinn moved close to her and covered her mouth with his hand.

"Why the children?" Blossom asked. I watched her holding the baby, and she seemed to enjoy it. After being around the twins, I guess it was nothing for her now.

"It's always the dang children," Taria sighed, shaking her head. Quinn let Toya go and moved to the bassinet to pick up Naheem.

"Honestly, I think they are looking for a certain child. Everything that I have gone through from my Pack that was written down is supposed to be a wolf shifter child or children born within the last six years. A wolf shifter that will restart the births of Dire-wolves," Quinn stated. I took in that information, figuring out exactly how that would work. It would need to start...

"Damon, are you going to get your shit together, or are we leaving your dumb ass here?" Toya rolled her eyes as she pushed by me. At least she tried to push past me, but that shit wasn't going down. "God, you are annoying. Taria, you are lucky I am going to indulge you with this request," Toya said, stepping around me.

"My bad. No need to be an asshole about it. You have such a Short temper," I said as she opened the door.

"Thank you, Toya," Taria laughed as Quinn handed her Naheem.

"Shani, where are the twins?" Toya gritted.

"Oh, oh, they are with Nuriel in their playroom. I will come with you to get packed, I guess, and help you get the twins situated. Taria, I am glad everything worked out okay, and congratulations to you both. I will get to know the babies when we get back," Shani smiled.

"Oh, Naheem says they know you well apparently, so no worries or something close to that," Taria said with wide eyes. We all looked at each other, but no one had a word to say.

"Okay, well," Shani laughed.

"I'm going with Shani," Lily said. She ran to Shani, and

they followed Toya out of the room. I watched as Blossom placed a now sleeping Ra'ah down before looking at the door. I looked back, expecting to see mighty mouth, but nothing was there.

"Well, let me get ready for this long-ass road trip, or are we using a portal?"

"Nope! We are traveling the good old-fashioned way. We have too much stuff to bring, and it is a lot of strain for LaToya if done consistently," Quinn said.

"Well, my Qu- Taria, I think I should get some things together for myself," Blossom said. Taria nodded as Blossom turned to leave. I knew something was up, but I could tell what, and those swirl of color eyes wouldn't meet mine. I didn't waste time saying anything else and followed the Shade out of the door.

I wasn't fast enough cause Blossom's ass was gone. I clenched and unclenched my fists, trying to calm myself. I smelled another scent that I knew had never been to this school before because I would have known it. I did know that I had smelled it before but only when I went to Sinful Secrets. It was another Shade, and I wanted to know why the fuck was it here. I shook my head and headed for my room at a speed no one could stop me. I didn't want to talk or answer questions from anyone. I made sure I had rooms far, far away from everyone else, and Taria had no problem making that shit happen. I wasn't stupid. I knew everyone knew about me and what I had done throughout my life. Not everyone knew the truth or believed it if they did, and I honestly didn't give two shits. I just wanted space to myself, but it was more that I didn't want to run into Blossom every time I turned around.

I made it to my side of the school and opened my door. I closed it, and the first thing I did was look around. I knew I wasn't alone, but I couldn't tell if the shit was in my head or in the damn room.

"Ashriel! Just say whatever it is you need to say or get the fuck out of my space," I growled. The only thing I received was silence, so I made my way to the bathroom. The light came on in the white marble room, and I stared into a mirror. I looked at myself, seeing everything I had done in the past on repeat in my head. It was hard and aggravating to deal with, but it was something else I had to bear. "Fuck it!" I growled as I opened the cabinet, grabbed a pair of scissors, and began cutting my locs.

"Things you have to deal with, Damon, will be hard to bear, but you chose this."

"I never said that I didn't choose it! I just want to know what exactly I am supposed to do? How can I help guide them if I don't know what exactly is coming?"

"You will know when it is needed for you to know. Right now, your one and only mission is to make sure they all survive. You are still one-half of yourself, Damon."

"I fucking know that! You told me that you would deal with that. That I would re-gain the half of my soul that was taken from me."

"When it is time, you will know how to get the other half of yourself."

"I wish you would speak with the sense God gave your ass!" I growled aloud. I waited as I clipped the last lock, but I heard nothing. I figured that was all I would get, so I wasn't mad. I looked in the mirror, staring at a reflection that looked more like my younger brother now. I opened the cabinet and pulled out the clippers. I lined myself up with a high-low fade and cleaned up my beard. I looked at myself again and saw some of the old me. Then the memories slammed into my thoughts again. Along with a voice, I thought, was long gone from my mind.

"I will bring you back, Damon Vaughn. Your soul will forever be mine!"

I slammed both fists on the marble sink cracking it in half as I roared. I did not know if that voice was the demon that controlled me or just the echoes of it coming back to show me everything I had done to protect my family. The memories showed me everything that would not gain me entrance into the afterlife with my family when it was my time to go. I would figure out where the other half of my soul is and take that shit back no matter what I had to do it get it. I just had to make sure Toya and her crew made it back here in one piece first.

"I will always do what has to be done."

I will do what I have to do, even if I have to deal with two creatures, a dog, a fake goodie-two-shoes, and a knee-high smart ass in heels.

CHAPTER 5
SHANI

I quickly followed after Toya, with my mind reeling at the news. I will be going with them on this trip. I knew I constantly hounded Quinn about not letting me go with them when the Pack would do things or when he sent our Pack members to handle situations that came up around the world. I wasn't a child. I graduated top of my class in every subject and excelled in close contact fight training. I loved the children. God knows I love them as if they were my siblings, but I wasn't just a babysitter.

"Surprised that you are going?" Toya asked. I blinked a few times and noticed that I had already caught up with her without knowing it.

"Well, yeah, I am, actually. I figure it's helping with the twins, but I am surprised because of what we might get into," I said. We made it to the end of the hall, and I smelled the most enticing scent. I looked around, but there was no one else in the hallway with us. It was weird because I knew I had scented it before, but my mind had to be playing tricks on me. We were not at Na'na's club, and I knew for a fact that I changed clothes and thoroughly washed the clubbing clothes before even stepping back on this side of campus. Liriel always thought I was going too far with it, but she hasn't been in this world long enough to understand that smells will get you caught the hell up in this place. Now we had to be doubly careful because that asshole Damon was living on that side. I shook my head, trying to clear it so I could focus on Toya.

"We will most likely get into something, I am sure, but you're not going just because of the twins, Shani. You will be eighteen in less than a month, and you have already finished school early. You are taking college courses as it is and still taking care of the children when we aren't around. You are a good kid that is rapidly becoming a woman. We have all noticed your skills in martial arts, the speed that you shift, and the power building inside of you. Your Alpha knows and sees that. Do you really think Quinn doesn't know what's happening around him? Especially his Pack?"

I looked at Toya as we made it to the front doors and passed by them to reach the other side. Toya and Quinn took up most of the rooms on the east side of the school's many dormitory rooms. I hated calling them that because they were more like a hotel suite than anything. Taria and Michael spared no expense when it came to this place. More like Taria didn't spare any cost, and Michael just let her do whatever she wanted. After all, she is Queen, so it is expected that everything would be overkill.

"Okay, so why am I going with you all, and what does my birthday have to do with anything?" I asked. I never celebrated that day because it was the day, the day my father died trying to save me, and the same day I lost my innocence.

"Well, that is something that you and Quinn will have to discuss, but I can tell you why you are going with us," Toya said as she stepped outside of the twin's nursery. She turned to me, looking up and smiling. She was so dang short it made me grin. "Stop laughing cause I gotta look up at your overly tall ass! It's not my fault that you grew into some kind of supermodel," she snapped. I stepped back as she tried to poke me in the ribs because she knew I was ticklish in that spot.

"I am not that damn tall! I'm only five feet and eight inches. You're just a bit on the small size," I laughed at the outrage on her face.

"I'm fun-sized, thank you very much!" She said as she flicked some burning embers at me.

"Hey!" I screamed as I patted my clothes. I looked up and saw her face become serious. It wasn't the regular crazy smart-ass Toya, but the one when we all found out that Taria was kidnapped.

"Shani, honestly, I didn't want you to come, and it isn't what you are thinking," she said quickly. I couldn't help the hurt that she must have seen in my eyes at that moment.

"Then why?"

"I didn't want you to come because I wanted to keep you wrapped up in a bubble with the twins. I didn't want what we were facing to touch you or my children. Quinn made me realize that it would do you more harm than good if we keep on shielding you from our crazy-ass world. He also made me watch every training session you had, so I could see that you weren't that little girl anymore. Taria and I look at you as our baby sister to shield you from everything that could hurt you. But I was quickly forced to realize that you are growing up and can handle yourself."

I moved because Toya had tears in her eyes, and I didn't want her upset about anything. Especially not me. I didn't want to cause her any more grief. If I had to stay back to make sure she didn't feel that loss again, I would stay here where it's safe. I leaned down and hugged her, and I felt her arms wrap around me tightly.

"I will stay and keep the twins with me. You and Quinn just do what you gotta do to get back to us," I whispered. Toya squeezed me once more before pulling back to look me in the eyes.

"No, baby, it's your time. I didn't know everything a wolf shifter goes through once they reach a certain age, but now I do. It's time that we let you be what you were meant to be. It's time for you to see what we are fighting so you can take your place next to us," she said as she wiped the tears from her face. I frowned because I had no clue what that shit even meant. I opened my mouth to ask, but she held up a hand, stopping me.

"That is something you and your Alpha will have to talk about in time. Just know that Taria and I are behind you one hundred percent. Just believe in yourself and your inner strength. You got this," Toya smiled as the door opened to the nursery. We both turned to see Nuriel looking at us with pink and blue paint all over his face.

"Little Witch, it is time that you take over your terrors...I mean, children. I need some peace and quiet," he said. I bit down on my tongue, but Toya laughed in his face. Nuriel was fine as hell on the worst days, but at this moment, he looked hilarious! He narrowed his eyes at both of us and then turned to smoke before drifting away.

"I wish I had that shit on camera!" Toya screamed.

"Shit! Shit!" Reign and Riaan giggled. They saw their mommy, and it was all over.

"Lawd, they will say that word for the rest of the day," she laughed. I was following her inside to help get the tiny creatures, as Damon calls them, together, so we could prepare to leave. "Nope! I got them. You go and get yourself ready to get out of here," Toya said, waving me off. I protested, but she wasn't hearing it at all.

"Fine, but I will be back to help you when I'm done," I said, closing the door.

~

Deadly Secrets

Before I went to my room to pack what I thought I needed, I wanted to tell Lireil what was happening. I had no clue how we became so close because our first meeting was rocky. I didn't like the way she was talking about Shannara to Jian at all, and I almost ripped her damn head off. If Sky hadn't stopped me, I might have done it. My emotions were out of control, and I didn't know the reason why I had so much rage. That was the first time Quinn had to sit me down and help me re-gain control over my wolf. I had no clue why the other half of myself seemed so volatile until he explained that it was normal. I passed my suite of rooms and went down another hallway where Lireil's rooms were.

I stopped just outside her door when that scent of cinnamon and chocolate hit me once again. I knew that scent because it was one I thought about constantly. *Tyson*. It was just on the edge of too sweet, but it wasn't. I looked around, but I saw nothing or no one around me. I blinked, letting my wolf peek out to see what I was missing or more like who the hell was following me. I knew it couldn't be the dude from the club. He didn't know who I was, and I prayed he didn't catch me watching him every time I went there. My gaze settled on the thick red curtains that hung from the large window. If anyone had passed by me, they would have looked at me like I was trippin for staring at a damn curtain. That was just it, though, because I wasn't looking at the curtain. I was looking at the man standing next to it. I knew that body, smell, and face that was attached to the eyes that were looking at me from head to toe. His head moved from side to side as if he studied me like a bug! His eyes at the club would sometimes be a glowing yellow, but they weren't his actual color. His eyes were damn near black unless they happened to flash burgundy. I only saw it happen a few times because I didn't want to get caught. I knew he would definitely tell Shannara if I did, and I couldn't have that happen.

Especially when she told me not to travel into the lower levels of the club, I couldn't help it, though, because I knew he would be there. It was just something about him, something my wolf wanted to scent, taste, and lick. I shook my head, trying to clear my thoughts. I looked at Tyson, the new Shade in charge of Sinful Secrets. "Do you hang around in the shadows, staring at everyone like that?" I snapped. I couldn't help the slight growl that left my throat. His brows raised, and a slow smile began to spread across his face. One minute he was in the shadows, and the next, he was in front of me.

"That's my job, *Comes Aminae*," he smirked. His accent was something I had never heard before, and I live around many species. Most of them were old as hell, and they all had slightly different accents, but his...his was different. I shook myself out of my head and looked up at him. I was tall, but I still had to look way up, and I was not feeling that shit at all. Toya always joked that I had Alpha energy, but I knew I wasn't an Alpha. It felt like something else, but I couldn't put my finger on it. I looked at his six-foot-three, maybe four frame up and down. His smooth dark brown complexion only made the burgundy that flashed in his eyes more pronounced. He was always dressed in black from his head to his black Timberland boots. He smirked at me again, showing straight white teeth that seemed sharp as hell. He raised a hand to smooth his low cut as he raised a brow at me. My eyes narrowed in an attempt to seem unaffected by his presence so close to me.

"What?" I said like a complete idiot. I shook my head as he took a step back. His smile never left his face as he took in a deep breath. "Whatever! Why are you following me?" I asked, crossing my arms. I could hear Lireil moving around in her room, so she must have heard me.

"Why would everything have to be about you? How would

I know that you were here? Am I supposed to know you or something?" He asked. I felt my canines poking me in my lip, so I tried hard as hell to rein my attitude back in and think for a minute. There was no way he would know who I was or that I would be here. But why was he watching me like that, and what the fuck was a Comes anime?

"What the hell is a Comes anime because that is not my name, nor am I a cartoon character. And I never said that anything had to be about me, but the fact you were just standing there looking at me like some kind of creeper says a lot!"

I was even more irritated when he laughed. I knew my aggravation would worsen because that laugh sent shivers through my body. I needed to get out of this situation because I knew I had been having problems lately with my body. That was the only reason I was in that damn club, anyway. If anyone found out or he put two and two together, that would be my ass. We both turned to the right when we heard voices coming in our direction. At the same time, I heard the lock on Lireil's door click. HE WAS IN MY PERSONAL SPACE before I could move or say another word, and his scent clouded my mind before his words sank into me.

"I did not say Comes anime." He chuckled. "I said *Comes Aminae*. But now isn't the time for all of that little wolf, not yet. I think you and your friend may not know enough to be in a club such as Sinful Secrets. Maybe you should stop while you're ahead."

This time I heard the word differently and could damn near taste the word on my tongue. I swallowed, but Tyson was already standing next to the window again. As Lireil opened the door, Marcus and Kahlil came around the corner.

"Tyson, what's up?" Marcus said, making his way toward us. I almost fell once Lireil pulled the door all the way open.

"Oh crap! Shani, what are..." Lireil stuttered. I caught

myself twisting around and pushing her inside of her room. "What the hell?" She shouted as I turned to slam the door shut. I didn't miss Tyson's dark gaze on mine before the door was shut firmly between us. I stood frozen as the rest of his statement hit my drugged ass brain. Who in the hell does he think he is to tell me what I should or shouldn't be doing? He doesn't know shit about me or what I have gone through! I let out a sigh and turned to face Lireil.

"Please tell me that isn't one of the dudes from the cl—"

I put my hand over her mouth and mouthed for her to shut up. I waited until she got the point before moving my hand out of the way. I dropped my hand and her brows bunched together before she shrugged like she was asking can she talk now. I put up one finger, moved over to the door, and listened for a moment. I took in a deep breath and scented the air before pulling the door open to double-check. I could actually feel that his presence was no longer there, but I had to be sure. Tyson, Marcus, and Kahlil were long gone now, so I closed the door and locked it.

"Can't you throw up a magical sound shield or something?" I asked. I was not taking any chances on someone walking by or ears listening in the damn shadows.

"Ahh, I can do something like that?" Lireil asked. She looked at her hands as if it would just happen automatically. I kept forgetting she was new to all the magic stuff, just like she keeps forgetting that everyone damn near can hear every damn thing around here. Not to mention smell where you have been or who you have been around.

"Yes. Well, at least once you learn how to do it. It's okay. We can talk in my room. Toya put a permanent shield on my room so I could have some kind of privacy. Let's go. I will need you to help me pack and tell you about the encounter in the hall," I said, pulling her with me out of the door. My mind was still racing from seeing Tyson so close up and having him so near me. I had to get the nerve just to tell him what I wanted from him. Shit, what I knew that I needed, but how? I may be turning eighteen soon, but I knew he would never look at me in that way. He had to be messing with me out there in the hall, and I wish I could get his words and voice out of my mind.

"Wait, wait," Lireil said as we headed to my room. "What do you mean pack? Are you leaving me in this place?" She asked. I got to my door and entered my code before I answered. My door opened, and I walked inside, finally feeling safe to get what happened in the hall off my chest.

"Yes, but close the door and lock it," I said, pulling off my white off-the-shoulder sweater. I was hot as hell and was glad I already had on a black tank top.

"Okay, where the hell are you going? I thought we were going to check out some colleges? You said you were thinking about going to NYU and wanted to check it out this weekend," Lireil questioned as she made herself comfortable on my bed.

"Yeah, well, not happening this weekend. Quinn wants me to go with him, Toya, Blossom, and Damon to take care of some Pack business and Toya's estranged family," I said, pacing.

"Wait! Damon? That crazy dude with the locks that be glaring at everybody? He taught one of my classes a few days ago, and one of the Werewolf boys, well, you know Monarae, right?"

"Yes," I nodded. That boy is an idiot to the fullest.

"Yeah, well, Damon threw him out the window! From the fifth floor," she laughed. I stopped in my tracks to look at her because why in the hell was Damon teaching any class?

"What class did you say this was again?"

"I didn't say which," she laughed. "But, it was Advance Physics." Lireil fell out laughing at the look on my face, and then I lost it.

"Wait, wait but, wait, why?"

"Girl! He yelled out the window that he was an idiot who would never learn a thing about motion in space and time when he couldn't even figure out it was TIME for him to shut the fuck up!" Tears rolled out of my eyes as we laughed for a good ten minutes at Damon's crazy ass. This was precisely what I needed to calm myself down. Lireil was good people like that. She always knows when to help me rein back my wolf. "Now that you are not trippin anymore, tell me what is happening," she said, wiping her eyes.

"Okay, okay, but was he really teaching, or are you playing me?"

"Oh hell no! He was really teaching, well, subbing, but it happened. Jian and I almost died laughing. I honestly think he did it because that asshole Monarae kept fucking with Jian, the entire damn class. But we can talk about that later. Tell me what's up," she waved.

"Okay, I will, and I will deal with Monarae's ass later. Anyway, I thought it was just for me to watch the twins, but Toya said it wasn't, and this is legit about me as a wolf. It's time for me to know my role in the Pack or which Pack I will go to once I turn eighteen. I always thought I would go back to the Rayne Pack, which would have been fine, but this is my family now. I love everyone here, especially the twins, Garrett and Lily. I want to be here. I'm nervous, and I don't know what to expect," I said in a rush.

"Well, first, I believe that Quinn would ask you where you want to be before just sending you anywhere. Pretty sure Toya wouldn't let that happen. So, did they say how long y'all will be gone?" She asked. I knew that I was one of the few people she hung around since getting here, and things still weren't great with Na'na, but it was definitely better. I moved to my bed and sat down next to her as she leaned against my headboard.

"I'm not sure how long, but I will let you know when I

know for sure," I said, and she nodded. "You are right about that. I didn't think about it that way. I mean, that isn't how things are supposed to be done, but you are right that Quinn would consider my feelings. Also, Toya wouldn't let it be any other way," I laughed.

"Good, now let's get to the real shit. Why was the sexy, crazy-looking dude from a BDSM club standing outside my door looking at you like a whole snack?"

I fell back onto my bed, covering my face with my arm. At least I could talk to someone about this cause I didn't think Toya or Taria needed to know where we had been sneaking off to on the weekends.

Before leaving Michael and Taria, I double-checked all three of the babies. None of us expected triplets, but here they were, and they were healthy. They were powerful as hell to be so young, but that was expected because their parents were just as powerful. As I held each child in my hands, I got a reading of their vitals and development. I had always been interested in becoming a physician but becoming the True Alpha has opened up so much power and gifts that now I see where the instinct to become one came from. I wanted to speak with that Druid a little more because I had to know what it was that I couldn't do to save my sister. I should have overcome any type of situation now that I honed my skills. I kept walking toward my wife and children just for a sense of normalcy before we started this journey. I took in a deep breath and smelled the faint scent of another Shade. I knew it wasn't Blossom and wasn't one I had contact with a lot.

"Quinn."

I turned to the voice as the Shade in question stepped out of the shadows.

"Tyson, I thought another Shade was here. What are you doing here?" I asked with a frown. I could scent Shani, but it wasn't strong. I could tell he had been around her at some point. Shani has been my little shadow for a minute now. I looked at her as more than a Pack member. She was more like a daughter to me. I wouldn't say I liked her scent being anywhere near the Shade, but...

"I keep asking everyone around here if they have seen Damon anywhere? I get the same damn answer. *'Who the fuck cares where he is?'* He told me the school, and that was it. I figured I could find his ass somewhere, but this place has too many scents," he said. I could tell he wanted to say something else, but I didn't dig. I had enough shit going on than to get involved with what he and Damon had going on.

"Damon has an entire wing on the other side of the school that isn't being used. If you go outside and cross the courtyard and go inside, you will find him," I said.

"Aight, damn, that's all they had to say," Tyson said. I gave him dap before I started back to where I was headed. I turned sharply to catch Tyson before he either disappeared or melted into the shadows.

"Tyson, let me holla at you real quick," I said, making my way toward him. I could faintly smell Shani, but it wasn't strong enough as if they had been together all that long. "We need to talk about Shani. Let's step in here," I said, pushing open the door to an empty office.

I stepped back out of the office, glad to know that we were on the same page about my little shadow. I knew what was what when it came to wolves and Mating, but she needed more time. I would damn sure make sure she gets it. Tyson nodded as he went in the opposite direction to find Damon's ass. I turned around sharply, catching him once more before he slipped away. "Hey! Tell his ass to be ready in a few hours and don't be late," I asked. Tyson nodded, looking as if he was lost deep in his thoughts.

"I got you," he said before stepping into the shadows.

I picked up the pace to get to my family. I could hear the giggles and the word "shit" before I got to the door. I shook my head because I knew they would be saying this all day if I didn't stop it now. I opened the door to complete chaos. LaToya was packing things the twins would need, and she already had three suitcases to the side. Riaan and Reign had toys flying all over the room as they sat in their high chairs covered in oatmeal.

"Thank God! What took you so long?" LaToya said, looking up at me. I choked because she looked like she had gone through the battle of her life. We agreed not to use any magic with the children when doing everyday things. They had to see that not everyone had the same abilities, and it wasn't needed all the time.

"Did you lose a battle with the baby powder?"

"Shut up, Quinn! Get your children!"

"My children. I thought they were our children?" I laughed.

"Dada! Shit! Shit! Dada," Reign said as she threw the bowl at her brother, who raised a chubby fist and stopped it in mid-air.

"See, your dang children. It's your turn. They have already eaten and have been changed. I put their clothes out already. I will take a shower and fix my hair," she said. I watched her march over to the twins while dodging flying cars, stuffed bears, dolls, and whatever else they had in the air. She kissed each cheek then turned to look at me. I smiled as she twirled a finger in the air, and she opened a portal and stepped backward.

"Hey! Hey, that is—," I shouted, but the portal snapped closed. "Cheating!" I screamed.

"Da, da, da, da, Dada!" Riaan screamed. I shook my head and moved at a quick speed to stand in front of them both. I let the red ring in my eyes grow brighter, and their little eyes got bigger.

"Alright! Clean it up and stop with the bad words," I said, not cracking a smile. Every single item went back into its place as they both looked up at me with faces of innocence.

"Dada mad?" Riaan whispered, and Reign's lip started to quiver.

"Daddy isn't mad," I said as I took each of them out of their highchair and set them on their feet. "Okay, let's get cleaned up and dressed so we can go on a trip," I said. Reign walked, and Riaan crawled behind me as I made my way over to the double doors leading to their room. I opened it to see LaToya standing there with her arms crossed as she glared at me.

"There is mommy!"

"Ma! Ma!" The twins screamed. Reign dropped to all fours, and they both raced to her, drooling.

"How in the heck did you do that? There ain't no way they cleaned all that up without you helping them," she sniffed but smiled when the twins made it to her feet. She leaned down, scooped up Reign, then Riaan, and held them on each hip.

"I didn't do anything to help. I asked the twins to put their toys away, and they followed instructions. You know the way you do when you don't want to get in trouble with daddy," I grinned.

"Oh my God," she laughed, turning away to head to the connecting bathroom. I followed her inside, and she handed me my son while she started to clean up Reign. Both of the kids looked at me, then at each other, and decided on something. Reign didn't whine, cry, or fight as LaToya cleaned her up, nor did Riaan as I got him together.

"You do realize that bringing them will be dangerous. We can leave them here with Kya and Kahlil. They would be fine."

"No, no, we need to take them with us. I know things will get a little crazy, but it shouldn't be too wild. You are just going to talk with Dax, and while I'm meeting the Witches and Warlocks in the Other realm, you will be with the kids. We need to spend as much time with them as possible. Look at them. They are growing so freaking fast," she sighed.

"Yes, but we know things do not turn out how we plan. When do we ever not run into some bullshi...mess?" I heard the knock on the nursery door and already knew who was coming inside. The doors flew open, and I listened to the angry march toward the bathroom.

"Yeah, it does, but I just don't feel like it will be a good idea this time. They need to be with us, and I can't tell you why. I just know it," LaToya said as she finished up with Reign and sat her on her feet.

"Aunt Toya! Why are you leaving me here? The twins get to go, but I can't? That is not fair," Kon said. His rainbow eyes glowed brightly as Reign wobbled her way over to him. Without a second thought, he reached down and lifted her into his arms. Reign dug her tiny hand into his hair and laid on his shoulder. LaToya turned to face the boy just as I finished up with Riaan.

"Kon baby, you have class, and you do not need to miss it right now. Plus, I asked Cam to take you and Garrett to any amusement park you want to go to this weekend," she smirked. She walked past him, kissing his cheek as he stood there with his mouth open. I held Riaan and stepped forward, making him snap out of his amazement and look up at me.

"Isn't that what you said you wanted to do when you saw the commercials? I mean, if you want to come with us while I do boring Pack stuff and your aunt talks to many Witches, then..."

"No! No way Uncle Quinn! I gotta tell Garrett! Does he

know about this? Wait! Wait, is Lily going?" He asked as he turned to follow LaToya.

"Nope! Just the boys. I hear even Uncle Marcus and Jian are thinking about going," LaToya said.

"I gotta go find Garrett while we have our hour break," Kon said, rushing Reign over to LaToya. Reign loved Kon, so her face scrunched up. "It's okay, RaeRae. I will come back before you leave," he promised as he kissed her on the forehead. She let her mommy take her as Kon ran out of the room, slamming the door behind him.

"How in the world did he find out already?" I asked.

"Probably Damon," LaToya growled. "Why are you letting him go with us? He doesn't need to go. Taria is just tripping because she has been out of it since the delivery."

"Because as much as you don't like him, our children love him, and he would do anything to make sure they are safe. Shani will be there, but she is going because it is time for her to know her part in this Pack. Also, I want her to meet a significant person. So, the more protection for you and MY children, the better I feel," I stated. LaToya looked up at me, and I knew she understood exactly where I was coming from and that this felt right.

"I will not be nice to him."

"No one asked you to be nice. Plus, I doubt he will be nice to you," I shrugged.

"Is what you believe happening with the Pack as bad as I think it is?" She asked. I stared into her eyes, thinking back to when I was just figuring out who and what I was on our last trip. It felt so long ago that it was basically a distant memory.

"Yes. And I think it has been happening for longer than I believed at first. I need to get rid of whatever is trying to attack my Packs before it can dig deeper. This time, Thomas Rayne will be the better choice to handle what is happening with the children. Dax has his new Luna, and he needs to make sure his

Pack is healing. He has enough brothers to spread the wealth," I stated.

"Well, we all have a part to play in this game called life, I guess. Let's hurry up and get ready to go. I need to find Nuriel and see why he feels the need that he has to take *"vacation time"* right now. I swear I think he and Katherine are going to be sneaking off somewhere for some private time," she groaned.

"Okay. I am going to go see what Mike is calling comfortable but safe transportation for our trip." I stated. "You go get yourself together, and I will take the terrible two with me," I said. I moved over to the corner and pulled out the double stroller.

"Yeah, you do that! Tell him to make sure it's big enough that I don't have to deal with that Demon he calls brother," LaToya said as she kissed both twins before walking her short ass out of the room.

~

Deadly Secrets

I ASKED a few Pack members to bring the twins' suitcases that LaToya insisted they would need down to the courtyard. I listened to Riaan and Regin babble to themselves as I pushed them to where Michael told me to meet him. I waited for the doors to slide open that would lead us to the giant garage that held every vehicle that was owned by all of us. When the doors opened, I could not believe what the hell I was looking at. The twins became louder as we made our way over to Michael. He stood there next to this enormous truck, speaking to Winston. I didn't know he was back already, but it was good to see him either way. Before I made it over to them, Michael turned to us and smiled at the twins. The twins started to shake the stroller, and I pushed it faster so they could see their Godfather.

"Reign and Riaan, where are you going?" Michael said, lifting them out of their stroller with a thought. They flew the rest of the way to him and laughed so hard they started to hiccup.

"Winston, when did you get back? I thought you were helping Delioness find the missing Lion shifters?" I asked.

"Yeah, we found a few but couldn't find any more locations. I figured we should regroup and see if we could find anything else out from Jason. Delioness wanted to check on a Lion shifter that the Rayne Pack saved. We only figured that out when Hayley said something about her, figuring she had to be one of the missing. We thought that maybe she could give the Lion Queen a clue to where others may be, so she headed that way when we parted," Winston explained. I looked at Mike, and he was walking toward us, holding both twins. They babbled at him the entire time before looking at Winston. They didn't know him that well, but I knew that would not stop them. They knew family, and Winston was family.

"Well, we are going there, so we will try to help if we can," I said as Reign damn near threw herself at him.

"Hey, hey! Hold up, what am I supposed to do?" He asked as she started slapping his bald head.

"Mike, what is this thing?" I asked, pointing to the giant truck. It looked like something the Military would use.

"It's what you will use while you take my Godchildren off this property," he said. I stared at him because who the hell was supposed to drive it? I mean, I could, but damn sure not Toya's short ass. I looked at it again and then back at him. "It actually has two stories, and it is fully loaded. It can hold up to ten people comfortably. It's definitely enough space for Toya and Damon not to be close to each other to get on your nerves. It will also give the twins enough..."

"Enough room to get into stuff, but I see what you mean,"

"Yeah, that, and it is just about fireproof. I knew this day would be coming, so I had this commissioned a while ago," he said, patting Riaan's back. Riaan was lying on his shoulder, falling asleep.

"You saw something I need to know about?"

"Nothing that I can say to you at the moment. As of now, if I do, it may change the outcome. I can see two endings that make me not want to say anything. I will call or reach out somehow if it can help at that moment. That is actually the reason Taria wanted Damon and Blossom with y'all," Michael said.

"Yeah, I feel you. We will probably go to Dax spot first, then figure out if we should head to New Orleans. I don't really want to, but LaToya has been dreaming of it lately, and things her father has told her about her family," I said, looking over the huge vehicle. I didn't notice that Damon's ass was inside of the truck until he opened the door and jumped out. "Tyson was looking for you."

"Yeah, I got up with him," he said before walking around the other side of the large custom RV. I raised my brows at Michael, and he just shook his head.

"I don't know if you will get that far, honestly. You may, but it isn't clear which path you should take. But this was more of a reason for me to make sure you all had something to travel in to handle the BS that would come your way. I feel like you may have a run-in with some government types."

"What? You got to be kidding me?"

"Naw, I'm not. We will do what we can, but they are fascinated with our children," Michael growled.

"They will be fascinated with seeing their head being ripped from their bodies if they come near my damn family," I grunted.

"Winston! Just give her to me! You are acting like you're

scared of a baby!" Damon yelled. Michael and I both turned to see Damon pluck Reign out of Winston's arms just as I heard the click of heels coming our way.

"I am sure the only thing he is afraid of here is your psycho behind!" LaToya shouted. She was with Shani and Blossom.

"What the —" Michael started, but I caught him looking down at Riaan, who smiled up at him. LaToya was her usual self, decked-out with some expensive ass heels, a tee-shirt dress, and a large belt. "You would swear she was going to a photoshoot," Michael laughed.

"The fact that this is probably what she considers casual makes it hilarious," I said before looking at Damon and Winston.

"No one is scared of a child, Damon! I was surprised, and I did not want to get my suit dirty," Winston growled. He brushed invisible dirt from his clothes before adjusting his cuff links. "Quinn, I hope everything goes well with you. I need to catch up on what I missed. Michael, I will see what's up with Derrick and find out where my sister is now. I am sure she is ready to join us here," Winston said.

"Yes, before you check in with Derrick, could you please check on Taria? She wanted to see you and introduce you to the babies."

"Babies! More than one," Winston said, with brows raised.

"Yes."

I saw the shock, then the realization that he had to see more kids crossed his face. He looked down at his suit with a slight growl.

"That will be my first stop," he said, spinning around.

"You wrong for that," I laughed.

"He is aight. He needs a little shake-up right now. The Lion Queen threw him off his game," Michael laughed.

"Just give me my child!" LaToya said. That brought me back to the vehicle.

"While they talk their usual trash, give Riaan to Shani and run this massive tank down to me so we can get moving.

"Bet. In the long run, I think you will appreciate it with you having to put up with that," he gestured to the bickering between Damon and LaToya.

"That is one thing you saw coming that is on point already," I laughed as he began giving me the rundown.

7 CHAPTER
LATOYA

When I saw this house on wheels, I was skeptical as hell. Michael thinking we needed this thing in the world is crazy as hell. All of that thought evaporated once we stepped foot inside this thing. It had everything we needed and a lot of things we didn't, but I was glad that we had another floor. The fact that I could go upstairs and away from Damon when he started talking his shit was perfect. I knew why Quinn wanted to drive first and have Shani sitting with him up front, but that left me with the idiot. I let out a sigh, knowing I needed to go back out there and talk to this fool. I was still upset that Nuriel claimed that he would meet me before I had to cross over into the other realm. I wanted to know what he had to do and what was so damn important that he couldn't be here now when I needed him. He was my familiar, but I realized it was much more than that. I had become reluctant to be without him if the voices came back.

I knew I had to deal with that shit on my own because he was not a crutch I could keep using. That is the actual reason that I was pissed off. I had to talk to Damon. He knew something about this gift of death magic that I hadn't even discussed with Quinn. I felt the change when we came back from Hell and its strength. That power was intense but also consuming, and I was slowly beginning to be afraid of losing myself. The voice that whispered in the back of my mind differed from the others and was more hateful but pervasive. "Fuck." I sighed again, opening the door. I looked back to the twins sleeping, then made my way out of the comfortable room I claimed was ours. There were only two rooms, but the one on the second floor had multiple beds and a T.V. The room on the first floor had a spacious bathroom, and the bedroom had a queen-sized bed with room for a small closet. I made sure I was steady on my feet before making my way toward the living area. Blossom was sitting at the booth-style table with both her legs up in the seat crossed. Her eyes were closed, but I knew she wasn't sleeping. Honestly, I wasn't sure if she even slept, but that was a convo for another time. Blossom's eyes popped open, and her colorful, swirling gaze met mine.

"Hey," she smiled. I remembered that she told me it took massive concentration on her part to track down Hell gates and that she was still doing so now. Lehana had managed to hijack them at one point, but just because she was now dead didn't mean they were entirely safe. Blossom said they were more than ninety percent safe as it stands, but it wasn't good enough if it wasn't one hundred percent. She devoted her time tracking down the remaining followers of Lehana that may still have a Hell gate to use.

"Hey, Bee. Can you chill in the room with the twins while they're sleeping for a few minutes? I don't want them in there alone while we are on the move," I asked.

"Yes, I can continue what I was doing in there. It's not a problem," she said.

"Thanks."

"No problem. I am sure the sleeping babies are more fun to be around than that over there," she said, scooting out of the booth. I couldn't help the glance I sent Damon's way when she stood up. Damon was lying on the couch playing with a phone, not giving us the time of day.

"I feel you. I would rather be next to anyone other than that," I smirked. I saw his thumb motion pause at my words before they started moving once more. Blossom wasted no time and went into the room, closing the door behind her. I made my way over to Damon and stood in front of him, waiting for him to look up.

"You finally feel tall now that you can look down at me, huh," he grunted. My eyes narrowed, but I wasn't about to let his asshole ways stop me from asking what I needed to know while I could.

"Shut up!" I snapped and reached down, slapping his feet off the couch so I could sit down.

"What a way to ask for a favor by assaulting the person you want to ask," he said as he repositioned himself. He typed out something before pocketing his phone. His gold eyes settled on my brown ones as if I was going to say sorry. Ahh, wrong chick if he thought that shit was happening.

"First, I don't need to ask you for shit because you offered. Unless you offer things and don't stand by your word," I smiled right back at his ass. "I will say nice touch with the fresh-cut and line-up, though. Those locks did absolutely nothing for you," I grinned.

"Oh, wait until I tell the dog how you are checking me out and shit. I knew you really had a crush on me. That's why you always gotta talk shit," he chuckled. It was deep, without humor, and I could feel the underlying menace in it. I squinted at him because I knew he wasn't all there from the jump. I didn't trust him entirely, but I trusted what he knew about death.

"Look, I don't like you, and I know you can't stand me, but I need to know what you were talking about earlier," I stated. I figured getting to the point would make the knowledge I needed come a little quicker. Damon leaned back while studying me as if he was deciding if he was even willing to help me with the shit. "Taria said that you were here to help, so fucking help," I gritted. Damon was in my face before I could even blink. His fangs were long as hell, and I felt the same fear as if I was back in that building he held me in until Quinn came for me.

"I ask myself why should I help you when you give me so much shit. Then I smell your fear when I get too close and taste the sweat that beads at your temples. That reminds me of what I did to you, and whether or not you believe the shit, I do regret it. Don't let yourself be fooled, though, because I would do that shit all over again if it were called for. So maybe you are right to fear me still. What I will not do is have you think that any of that shit was willing on my part. If you want help, you will either need to get over it and move on or keep holding onto my fear. Hold on to that fear of death that you believe will happen at my hands, or let it go and move the fuck on. Your choice! Make it now!" He growled.

I was shaking and knew he could feel it, but my spine turned into steel and hardened with his words. I felt the boiling rage I held and my power burn inside of my body as if I could set this entire fucking world on fire. I felt the knowledge that I was no longer vulnerable the way I was that night. I looked up as I realized I had removed my gaze from his, afraid that he would kill me at any moment. Deep, deep down, I knew Quinn was right, and I did trust him on some kind of level because I trusted my children around him. Even though I was still afraid of Damon from that night, it was more because I felt I was the same person who had no power to defend myself. That was no longer true, and the person, more so the Witch that I am today, wouldn't have backed down. The Witch I am today didn't run scared from shit! I knew the flames that lived inside of me danced in my eyes as I stared back at him. His fangs receded, and a slow smile spread across his face. "There she is, that's it, Toya. You've passed the first lesson already. Faster than I thought, so this may go better than I expected," Damon said, pulling away from me. I felt the pressure of his power and gaze fall away like shedding skin. I blinked, trying to figure out what he meant by his words.

"Wha-what?" I stumbled over my words before shaking my head, trying to cool the fire that lived inside of me. "What are you talking about?" I asked, frowning at him. Damon already had his phone out, but his gaze flicked up to meet mine for a second.

"The first step in controlling any kind of Death magic, LaToya, is overcoming the first thing that made you fear death in the first place," he answered as the vehicle came to a stop. Damon was on his feet in the next second, moving to the doors before looking back at me. "The rest of this shit is harder to overcome than that. It's all good, though, because I know you have what it takes to make this Death magic shit bend to your *Will*. Just, just don't tell anyone I said that bullshit," he growled before pushing open the door and exiting the vehicle.

"What the fuck?" I whispered as I turned inward. I began to focus on this new feeling that seemed to awaken inside of me. My eyes flew open when I found access to a power that burned hotter than any flame I had ever produced. I looked at the open door and shook my head. "This does not mean I like your bitch ass," I whispered, knowing he heard every word.

~

Deadly Secrets

I didn't know we had been on the road that long until I stood and looked out the windows. The first thing I saw were people everywhere. I looked closer and could tell they weren't just people but shifters. That's when I realized that we had to be at Dax's house. I turned when Blossom opened the door to peek her head out.

"He is gone, right?" I looked around and turned back to her, trying not to laugh.

"Ahh, I am pretty sure you know his ass is already gone. What's up with you?" I asked. She looked back in the room before stepping out and closing the door. Her eyes moved as if she was taking everything in before she began sniffing the air.

"There are more than wolves here. That is interesting," she said, ignoring my question.

"Hey!" I said, shaking my head. Blossom rolled her eyes before shaking her head.

"Yes, he just," she looked away with a slight growl.

"Oh, I get it," I said, laughing as I raised a hand, shielding ourselves away from all the ears if they were listening. "Okay, say whatever it is you need to say. It's fine. Give me the tea," I grinned.

"I, ahh, don't have any tea, but if– "

"No, no, girl. Just tell me what's up with you and him," I laughed.

"Oh well, I don't know, and that's the problem. I think I see what you and Taria were saying. I did the whole flirt thing you said to do, but he...he's a child. To me, he has lived a fleeting time compared to what I have lived. That would make me a...a..."

"A cougar and ain't nothing wrong with that!" I laughed.

"Well, I don't have time for it. There is a war, and I need to focus on that and my Queen," she stated. I knew enough not to push the subject, so I let it end at that.

"How about we deal with whipping some bitch Witches and Warlocks into submission," I said. I watched as the swirl of color went jet black as she smiled, showing the tips of her sharpened teeth.

"Yess, yes, that I can do."

I laughed and waved a hand and then heard Hayley calling me outside.

"Reign and Riaan are still sleeping, but I can feel that they are about to wake," Blossom said. I nodded and headed for the door. I saw the first person when I stepped out, Hayley, and she was glowing.

"Hey, girl! I wanted to stay after the wedding, but I had to tell my brother the news," she smiled.

"You're pregnant! Oh my God! You're having a baby!" I screamed, and she hugged me.

"I know. I know I need to get back and tell Taria as well. I want to see those babies too! Camron seemed stunned when he called me."

"Yeah, we all were losing it, but it turned out for the best."

"Yes, I am so glad about that. I wanted to be there, but I needed to speak to Dax about some other Pack business."

"Something wrong in Florida?"

"No and yes. I want to either send another Alpha for the Pack in Florida or let them come here. They have been through so much, and they need to see what a functional Pack looks like," she sighed.

"You spoke with Quinn about this? I think he will say to let them come here with everything that is going on with the children," I said.

"Yes, it was decided that we should call a Pack meeting, so I know Quinn is seriously thinking that way as well," Hayley said. I looked past her and saw Shani standing next to Quinn as he spoke to Dax and a woman with lavender eyes. I think her name was Maeze, and from what Quinn had discovered, she was related to Shani.

"Are you going to stay for the meeting?"

"No, I need to get back to Cam before he does something to piss off Michael. We need to see his parents and tell them as well. I was hoping you could open a portal so I can get back faster," she said, smiling. I could see how happy she was, but something flashed in her eyes. It almost looked like sadness.

"You know I got you, girl," I said, stepping back. I felt a hand on my shoulder and turned to look at Blossom. I will take her back myself. The twins are waking up," she said. I gave Hayley another hug, then went to get my babies and get this show on the road. After changing Reign and Riaan, I decided to eat a little before getting them around everyone. I knew once they saw other children, they would not sit still.

"Hey, need help?" Shani asked. After getting Riaan seated in his booster seat, I looked up to see the girl looking shell-shocked.

"Sure, what's up with you?" I asked as I began feeding Riaan, and she fed Reign.

"Nothing, just sensory overload, I guess. I didn't expect to miss this place and Pack so much or think I was missed at all," Shani stated quietly.

"Of course, but that isn't all of it. What's up," I asked? I gave Shani all of my attention and waited for her to start speaking.

"It is a woman here that was not here when I left. She is actually related to me, and I never thought I would meet anyone connected to my father by blood. From what has been said, she will be my new trainer. It's great, don't get me wrong, but," she trailed off. I finished up with Riaan and reached out for her hand.

"I haven't met her in person, but Quinn would not choose someone he didn't trust to help you further your training. Also, it will give you time to know more about your father's side of the family. Come to think of it. I don't know that much about your parents. Is..."

"Oh! Crap, I forgot to tell you that Journee said she really needs to speak with you," Shani said suddenly. She stood up and picked up Reign in one smooth motion. I looked at her but decided I would corner her ass later about that evasion tactic.

"Let's get to it before that meeting," I said, grabbing my baby and following Shani out of the RV.

When stepping out, I immediately noticed the Rayne brothers and good lawd! I didn't let a word slip from my lips because I knew everyone had excellent hearing and Quinn was not about to kill me so soon on this trip. Dax noticed us, and I completely understood what Taria's ass was talking about when she first saw him in person. I find it hilarious now because I couldn't see any of them as nothing more but older brothers.

"Damn Damon, I heard the saying to Hell and back, but I didn't think you would do that shit literally," Malic laughed. I scrunched my face up as Malic walked toward us from the house with a huge grin. It almost seemed like these two were friends or some shit.

"Well, I made it back, didn't I?" Damon laughed as they gave each other dap.

"Oh God, you got to be kidding me," I said, rolling my eyes. Quinn turned to look at me, and that's when I saw Journee standing with another wolf. The white hair in the front told me that had to be Dimitri, Dax's Beta. His energy, though, was strange. It felt almost akin to my own like he had a little Witch in his blood.

"Don't mind the vertically challenged people. Have you asked anyone about the problem yet?" Damon laughed as Malic leaned back with a shut the hell up look on his face. I ignored them and made my way over to Journee. She caught my gaze and smiled, almost in relief. That caught my attention, and I knew I had to speak to her quickly. I turned back to Shani, "hey can you take the children and get them situated with the other kids? I need to talk to Journee for a few," I asked.

"Yes, that's a good idea anyway cause I think the meeting

will be soon," she said. I put Riaan on his feet as Shani took the twins by the hands and led them to the other children shifters playing. I turned back just as Journee made her way over to me and I embraced her once she became close.

"I am so glad you are here. You do not know," Journee sighed.

"Why, what's up? Whatever it is, we can figure it out," I said. We began walking as she told me everything about what had happened to Peter and his family.

"I don't know. I just get the feeling we missed something. They were on some demonic shit and I can't move on from this until I figure it out," Journee said.

"Peter Johnston and his entire bloodline were wiped out, correct? All of them including his sister, nephews, and her husband and his younger brother Gregory," I confirmed. Journee stopped in her tracks, looking at me oddly.

"What younger brother? What are you talking about?"

"His youngest brother. Peter's father died, but his mother remarried and had another child, which makes him Peter's younger brother," I stated. The frown on her face and clenched fists told me that she didn't know, and apparently, neither did Dax.

"Shit! They rounded up everyone who was at that house, Toya. They were the only people who were there and were expected to be there," Journee said, pacing.

"Okay, okay, the first thing is we need to find him and figure out if he did know anything about what Peter and the others were up to," I said. I pulled out my phone from the hidden pocket in my dress and detailed Annalise. I held up a finger for Journee to wait because I already knew what she was thinking. The decree came down on Peter's family, but Gregory wasn't technically a Johnston.

"Hey, Anna, when you were sharing the knowledge of the other Circles, we came across the Johnston family."

"Yes, I remember. It was Peter and his sister, but they had a younger brother. He lived with the father, if I am not mistaken. His father is a Knox Beaumont, and he belongs to the Beaumont-Baylor Circle. Do you want me to contact them?"

"Naw, no, but can you text me over a number and address for them, please? Do we know what side they are on things?"

"Baylor has as much pled their Circle without saying so. We managed to save one of the members from Valerie when she took hostages. Two of their children attend school here, but the Beaumont side seemed to have distanced themselves from Baylor. . The La Beau Pack never dealt with either family unless necessary, but it wasn't bad blood. The Beaumont Pack haven't taken a stance of who they pled their loyalty to either way, " Annalise stated.

"Okay, well, we shall see what's what, I guess."

"I'm sure you will figure it out. I will send everything to you right now."

"Okay, thanks."

I ended the call and looked up at Journee. "It's all good. We will figure that out before we leave, so don't worry," I smiled.

"Yeah, I know. I just hate that feeling, you know. Like something being left undone and the feeling that something will happen," she gritted.

"I get it, and we will take care of that shit as soon as this meeting is over," I said, leading her back to everyone else. I left Journee and went over to Quinn, still knowing something wasn't right here and thinking about that name. When I heard it before, I thought the same thing but never looked into it any further. Everything that happened to Taria, trying to figure out how I knew a name was the last thing on my mind.

"Hey, Toya. Thank you for sending Journee when y'all did," Dax said.

"No problem, I am always here to help. I would rather have someone I know taking care of y'all anyway. I do have a quick question, though," I said. I felt Quinn's arms around my waist and I knew he was picking up on the tension I was suddenly feeling. Journee was right, and something was up.

"What's up? Whatever I can answer, I will, and what I can't, I am sure someone can," Dax stated. His violet eyes seemed to glow as he waited for me to say something. The way his huge body shifted, I could tell he may be picking up on the same thing.

"Peter Johnston. Did you kill everyone connected to what he was up to?"

"Hell yeah," he said, looking at me and then Quinn. I knew all the details because he told Quinn everything that went down.

"Did you or anyone else here know that he had a younger brother? He may or may not have any involvement in what happened, but something isn't sitting right with Journee or me," I stated. I felt Quinn's hand clench around my waist because this just couldn't be a simple stop and chat. Something had to happen because that is just how our life moved. Dax stared at me for a long moment and didn't move when he called over his shoulder for Dimitri.

"What's up?" Dimitri asked, looking at all of us.

"Did you know Peter had another sibling?" I saw the frown and confusion from Dimitri before he spoke.

"Naw, no, since when? I have never known them to have another–" Dimitri stopped and looked at me.

"He has a younger brother named Gregory," I stated.

"That had to be on some underground shit, or he was never around here at all. Peter nor his sister never said a word," he said, looking at Dax. We all were thinking the same thing, and that was if he was still alive. Was Gregory a part of the same bullshit as his brother and sister? And where the fuck was he now?

CHAPTER 8
DAMON

I followed Malic as we all went to The Pit, and I realized that I hadn't had so many dogs in my life surrounding me like now. The school had many, but not as many as this, nor are they this powerful. I was cool with all the brothers and was lucky they were not the type to hold grudges like Toya's ass. I guess it was more they knew me from before or heard the story of what happened.

"So what's up with the sexy woman, Shade, y'all got along for the ride? I did not know they made them like that!" Malic smiled, and I almost put my hand through his rib cage. I checked myself because I knew that Malic knew my feelings on the Shade matter. He was fucking with me, just like I would be doing. If it weren't for him, I wouldn't know about the pixie dust that would help me do what I needed to do about Blossom. I wouldn't deny the sexual tension between us, but the fact that I knew she believed that I couldn't handle her power was laughable. *She must not know me as well as she thinks.*

"Don't make me choose to forget that I like your punk ass. Leave the Shade out of your mouth," I growled low. His smirk told me everything, and I knew I had to stop this shit right here and right now. He was worse than me, and I knew he would keep going.

"I mean, I would be willing to show her around and what it's like to get out of Hell," Malic grinned. I stopped as people moved around us and raised my voice.

"I didn't think you had time for all that when you claim to be getting kidnapped by birds and shit," I said as Max came up on our left. He stopped, looked between Malic and me, then frowned.

"What? Who is being kidnapped by birds?" Max asked. He was louder than me, and there wasn't a need for all the exceptional hearing that surrounded us. It made it funnier to me. Malic's eyes narrowed at me, and I just smirked.

"Both of y'all shut the fuck up. Damon let it go. I told you about that in confidence," Malic growled.

"Told him what? I'm your brother! Your twin brother at that! Damon, what happened?" Max asked, but then a fine as hell woman dressed head to toe in black leather pushed past us. I knew she was a Hunter just by how she moved and eyed me. "Nevermind. Malic, we will talk about this later. Dali, Dali baby, you could speak when you see me," Max said as he followed the Hunter, who seemed to roll her eyes at him. I noticed that she inched closer to him simultaneously, so it wasn't a one-sided attraction.

"I will leave the Shade alone. Just keep the Owl quiet, damn. And it didn't kidnap me, it just...just picked me up. Anyway, we need to get on with this shit," Malic gritted. He turned away and moved to stand next to his younger brother Thomas, flanking him on his left side while Max took up the right side after making sure the Hunter was sitting directly in front of him. I looked behind me because I picked up on hushed whispers, but the smell of tears is what got me. I took a step back, finding myself in the shadow of the building that was called *The Pit.* I tensed when I realized Blossom was standing next to me.

"Oh, so now you want to be close to me? It didn't seem like you had any convo for me on the ride here," she said. Blossom's arm brushed against mine, and the heat that raced through my body told me I had to get this Shade out of my system. I just needed one time, and then I could think clearly. Just once.

"I had a lot I wanted to think about," I gritted. I moved slightly, so we weren't so close. Her scent was driving me insane and I knew if I spoke to her on the way here, I would have said fuck it. Toya would have come out of that room to see her friend bent over that fucking table. I closed my eyes, trying to push that shit away because this is not why I am here. She is not what I should be focused on right now.

"Funny. Maybe I wasn't wholly wrong earlier, ***Jovetoto***," she murmured, more to herself than to me. I frowned because I know damn well, she did not just call me a youngin! Hell naw! I moved before she could register it and had her back pressed against the cement wall as my hand came to rest at the base of her neck.

"Don't mistake me deflecting your tries at flirtation and comebacks as I am weak or young. People always seem to make that mistake thinking that I don't know what I am doing or I am out of control. You feel this shit just as much as I do, but what you will understand is when the time is right, I will take you up on all you throw out. You may be older than I am, but I have the experience, *Zaila*," I growled. I could taste her breath as she panted under me. I could feel her heart beating rapidly for her kind. The swirling color of her eyes bled to full red.

"How do you know that name?" Blossom growled out in a whisper. I let the hand resting on her throat tighten slightly, and the moan that escaped her only made me harder.

"I know everything I need to know when it comes to you," I grunted. Blossom brought her hand up, and it snaked around the back of my neck. I felt the tips of her sharpened nails as they dug into my skin. She pulled my face forward so close I was tempted to lick her lips until she let me inside.

"Then you must know that I am much stronger than you will ever be," she snarled. I felt her release me as she melted into the shadows. My hand came out automatically, catching myself before I fell into the wall. I couldn't help the satisfaction that I had gotten under her skin, and now she knew for sure what I wanted.

"Only for the moment, Shade."

I turned back around as the furious whispers became louder, and my eyes narrowed into the darkness. I saw the Witch that Toya had saved from that crazy bitch who killed her mother. She was talking to a young boy, which Toya saved as well. I cocked my head to the side as I let the other voices fade and focused on just them.

"I want to go home! Why do we have to stay here, mom?"

"Zaccai, this is our home now. This is our chance to start over with good people. Do you think Toya would let us come here if she didn't trust them?" Journee said. I could tell her patience with the conversation was running out. It seemed that it wasn't the first time, and I knew it wouldn't be the last. The boy was strong-willed, and I could feel how powerful he would become under the right circumstances.

"No, no, I like Ms. Toya, but I hate it here! Everyone is fine, and I like the other kids. It's, it's,"

"What is it, Zac? Just tell me, and I will fix it. You know what? Maybe after this meeting, we can sit, and you can tell me everything that is bothering you. If it's your magic, Dimitri and I could—"

"That's it! Him! Why is he always around? I just want my daddy back not, not him!" Zaccai stormed away and then started running toward the main house. I looked back at the Witch as she watched her son with her hand over her mouth. I only wanted to deal with the half-pint when necessary, but she needed to speak with her Witch. I moved away from the shadows and made my way into the pit just as Quinn stepped forward and began talking.

~

Deadly Secrets

I MADE my way to the back so that I could watch everything around me. Toya and Shani sat in the front as Quinn commanded attention. I saw his growth even if I wouldn't admit it to anyone. Without a word, he grabbed everyone's attention, and I could see the excitement in the faces of the wolves seeing the True Alpha in person.

"So, this isn't our first meeting, but this is the first time that you will witness changes that should have been made long ago. Dax Rayne is the Alpha of this Pack that includes the entirety of Maryland, but it will now include Maryland, Virginia, the District of Columbia, and Delaware. That is a large area for just one Alpha I know," Quinn stated. His eyes connected with each member as he spoke. Not all werewolves, but they all respected him as their Alpha. I saw Blossom standing at the opposite end of the pit, but she wasn't watching Quinn. She stared at another woman with teal-tipped hair and large teal eyes. I frowned because once I focused on her, I could feel the same pressure I would get from Blossom and my grandmother Selena. This creature was old, more like ancient, which confused me. Why would she follow an Alpha?

"Alpha, may I speak?" A female wolf said, standing. Her deep brown eyes with a ring of yellow set off the dark brown of her skin as she pushed the light brown hair from her face.

"Yes."

"How will that work? How do we trust these new wolves to join our Pack with everything happening? After everything with the rogue, we just became settled," she said and sat back down just as fast.

"Nieve, you are not wrong about feeling that way. I understand what you all went through not that long ago, but you all don't seem to realize that you are surrounded not by only one Alpha but six of them, and they are all-powerful," Quinn said. "Not only that, but you have other shifters here that are powerful as well, and with that power, there is nothing that can't be accomplished," Quinn stated. The mummers that he was correct started to filter through the crowd, and I saw the change in the brothers at his words. "This will not happen all at once, but this is what I task for Dax to do and bring all of this together while Thomas holds it down here," Quinn said. I saw the moment Thomas realized what Quinn was saying.

"Alpha, how is that different from any other time I hold this Pack when my brother has to handle business? I don't mind traveling to make your vision happen," Thomas said, confused. Dax looked satisfied about something, so I figured he and Quinn already expected this outcome.

"I know you would, but I need you for something else, Thomas, while you are here. The Pack in Florida, where I lived, needs a place. They need an Alpha to help them heal and show them the true way a Pack should be. Hayley took up the first half of that task, but I need you to complete it," Quinn said, holding his attention. "I think you and Remi are the right choices to handle this situation," Quinn said. He turned away from Thomas and missed the look he gave Remi, who, I guessed, was the teal-eyed woman. She looked like she was about to contest but closed her mouth and leaned against the wall. "Whatever is happening seems to happen with our children, so we need to pull in until it can be figured out. We all have a part to play, which is just the beginning. Anything that thinks it can attack any of my wolves will not make it out of this alive, especially when they target our children! I am here to tell you all that we as Alphas will end this threat to our nation, and it will start here!"

I felt the energy shift, and I saw the moment Toya noticed it as well. She stood as Quinn kept talking and made her way to the exit. I followed the little person to ensure she didn't get her ass caught up in something.

"Why are you following me, Damon?"

"Who said I was following you? It's harder to follow the short ones when you are always looking over their heads," I chuckled.

"Fuck you," Toya said, but the heat she usually puts into it was lacking.

"So you feel it as well? The death, the dark magic being used?" I responded. She flicked her eyes at me before facing forward once more.

"You would be the only other one who could feel evil," she smiled. The click of her heels was soft after we hit the pavement. I agreed with her because she was right. I could feel it, and it was intense. Too fucking strong and I felt the same eerie feeling as before.

"Did Blossom ever tell you the entire story of Halloween?" I said as I spotted something in the trees lining the property.

"She told me how you let the kids fight!" Toya snapped. But I ignored her because I knew what it was I was sensing.

"So she didn't tell you all about the cicada-looking bitches?" Her head snapped to me with a disgusted look.

"Bugs! Those nasty ass bugs? The ones that come from under the–" her words died off as the screaming started.

"Yup! Those are the ones! They are actually called ***Akhkhazu.*** I know of no wards that could keep them out if they dig deep enough," I shouted.

"Well, you will!" Toya roared as giant Jeepers Creepers-looking bastards crawled their way out of the ground.

"The children! They always go for the children!" I growled. Everyone in the pit was either shifting or taking them on in their human form. I already knew for a fact that more and more would keep coming unless we dealt with the magic-user responsible. I moved to try to flank Toya as flames danced along her arms and the markings flared red on her skin. Fire shot from her hand as she burned the first creature that came at her head-on. I reared back, using my right hand to slam fist first into one bug that headed towards the house. My arm went through its head and the nasty smell of death burned my nose. I pulled back, yanking out the rotting insides of this thing only to see it was a spine. It was the human spine of someone long dead. This was someone strong in magical ability, but dealt with death like a toy, and didn't care about the consequences. This Witch or Warlock danced on the edge of Necromancy, which only spelled out disaster.

"We need to find who controls them, or they will keep coming!" I screamed to Toya, but she was gone.

Chapter 9

Quinn

I felt something was off when I announced that Shani, who is from the Rayne Pack, would be joining the Savir Pack as my Delta. That's when I felt something off. I didn't feel it through my wolf's senses, but the part of me that is connected with LaToya. The Twice Marked part of me felt the magic being used, and it was evil. It was something I had never felt before, but nothing like what we faced in Hell. I saw when LaToya got up from her seat, but I thought nothing about it and wasn't worried because Damon followed her. My eyes snapped to Dax, who was looking into the distance, and I knew he felt something that should not be on his land.

"What the hell is that?" Someone growled before screams ripped through the air, causing everyone to go on full alert. I was already moving, thinking about my kids and if LaToya was in danger. I felt her rage and disgust, and I knew she was okay.

"Dax! The children! I want you with the children in case it is a diversion," I ordered and took off.

I was outside in a blink, knowing my orders would be followed. I could hear Dax directing his wolves to where they needed to defend with practiced ease. I wanted to get to my twins, but I knew stopping this shit right now would better protect them. The sight that greeted me was straight out of a fucking nightmare. I remember Blossom and Damon's full detailed report on Halloween, but this looked worse. I could hear LaToya screaming and saw a blaze of fire light up the sky. I took a step, shifting into the third form where it was easier to draw on the Twice Marked bond we shared. The heat of fire raced through my veins as I leaped into the air and landed beside Malic. He already had one of these bugs in a headlock, and I watched as he ripped its head clean off.

"I fucking hate bugs! Nasty pieces of..."

Malic was cut off as the ***Akhkhazu*** stood back up as another head took its place. I didn't wait for it to fully regrow before I shoved my fist through its chest and pulled out the rotting remains of a glowing yellowish-green heart. I squeezed the heart, let a power burst flow through, and burned it to ashes. The body dropped to the ground, and Malic jumped back, looking at it as if it had bitten him. "See, this is why I never watched that fucking movie! That shit is real as fuck! Got damn Jeepers Creepers looking monsters," he growled as another man cicada-looking thing climbed its way out of the ground and grabbed his legs. If these bugs held sacrificed human hearts, they would be stronger than the ones Damon fought on Halloween. That's when I felt the magic in the air and heard the buzzing and chittering sounds increase. The body of the bug I just took out began to shake, then slid up boneless. Its eyes opened and I stared into the flat black eyes as it smiled. All I saw were needle-like teeth before they charged at me.

"What the fuck!" I growled. I caught the thing in the air, and then I was attacked by another one from the side. I saw Malic clawing at the dirt in front of me, but more and more ***Akhkhazu*** came at me.

"I know damn well Damon brought these things here cause he knows I hate fucking bugs!" Malic roared as he shifted. I could tell by doing that, it changed how the bug was holding him. He managed to get out of the hole as I ripped the head off the ***Akhkhazu*** and threw one into the three coming from the right side of me. I sensed another predator, and it wasn't one from this Pack. It was coming from above, and I looked up briefly. I saw something that I believed had died out over a hundred years ago. An enormous Owl dropped down from the dark sky and used its massive claws to attack two bugs, ripping them into pieces. Malic shifted back and looked up as another bug began piecing itself back together. Its leathery skin stretched and pulled until they were just as ugly as before. "See, I told y'all that—" Malic's words were cut short when the owl dropped down again and scooped him up, taking off back into the sky.

"Hell naw! Put me down, put me down now!" Malic roared, but he was already far into the distance.

"What kind of shit is going on here?" I grunted. I didn't have time to waste thinking about it. Malic would be okay because it didn't seem like the owl wanted to hurt anyone here or him. He is an Alpha, so I knew he could get away if he wanted. Something wasn't right because destroying the heart should have done the trick and lessened the numbers.

"LaToya!"

"Baby, I am going for whoever is doing this! If we stop them, then all of these nasty bastards will fall."

"I feel you on that, but something isn't right. I burned a hear, and that thing returned, and so did others."

"We are having the same issue. That's why I am trying to get a lock on the bitch threatening our people!"

"Make sure Damon is with you! I will stay close to the children."

"I am about sick of y'all telling me to keep a demon close to me. One that tried to kill me, I might add."

"LaToya!"

"Aight, all right! It is not like he is not following me around like the stalker he is, anyway. Keep the babies safe, Quinn, and don't forget about Shani!"

The connection was stopped, but her words had me scanning the area while the ***Akhkhazu*** began pulling themselves back together again. I started to burn each piece as I sensed Shani and saw her fighting back-to-back with the Shade. I moved to make my way over to them, figuring out what we were missing. I ducked and came up with my claws extended, grabbing an ***Akhkhazu*** by the throat. I dragged it behind me as I kicked the heads off of the ones coming from under the ground.

"Shani!" I shouted. She turned toward me with flashing metallic gold eyes, caught the ***Akhkhazu*** by the shoulder, and threw it with such force that it slammed into a large tree, snapping it. "Watch out!" I yelled at Alex, who was stomping one bug back into the ground while beating another with an arm from one who was getting back up. Alex looked up just as the tree fell, and he used the ***Akhkhazu,*** who just stood up as a bat. He dropped the arm, picked up the bug, and slammed it into the trunk before leaping out of the way. I felt sharp claws on my arm as I threw the bug down in front of Blossom and Shani.

"Quinn! What the hell?" Shani said, jumping.

"Shani, don't kill it. We need to figure out why these things are regenerating themselves," I said. I looked at Blossom as her swirling eyes turned a deep crimson before she raised her sword in the air that seemed to transform as it sucked in all the light surrounding us.

"I will buy us a few minutes," Blossom stated before she roared. Blossom began to move, and it looked like a dance as she connected with every cast shadow. I watched as bodies started to form out of the shadows, with burning red eyes appearing behind every ***Akhkhazu*** except the one I held down under my foot. As Blossom moved, so did each shadow, and they all raised their blades in the air and struck down, sending out a shockwave of power that blew each of them apart. Body parts with leathery skin needled teeth, and beady red eyes were all over the place. The shadow people turned as one to Blossom before fading back from where they came.

"That was the coolest shit I have ever seen," Shani said with wide eyes. I raised a brow at Blossom when she looked at me. Her swirling, colorful eyes were back, and she smiled.

"I got the idea from Garrett. He will be a superior tactician of war when he is older. Now, let's figure out why these bitches won't stay down until Toya finds the Witch or Warlock that's doing all this," Blossom stated. She squatted down next to the only surviving Cicada, and the beady red eyes rolled to look at her before the buzzing started.

"I honestly believe that he came up with that, but why the fuck won't these shits die?"

I punched a hole through the chest and pulled out the beating yellowish-green heart. Thick red veins covered it as it beat wildly.

"That isn't like the ones we fought before. The heart looks like this when they are in Hell, meaning the one behind this is powerful—also working with some demonic magic. Almost akin to Necromancy," Blossom murmured. My eyes narrowed at that word. I read all about their asses when Michael told me about the island. I looked down at the bug, noticing that it was re-growing its heart while I still held the other heart in my hand. How is that possible? How many people have been sacrificed to animate this shit?

"Alpha!" I turned to see Dax and Devanna making their way over to me. I crushed the heart in my palm, then let the fire burn it until it was dust.

"The children?" I said, turning to them.

"They are fine. Thomas and Remi are protecting them inside the house. Is it over? What the fuck is this?" Dax asked. His violet eyes burned with anger and confusion. I knew what went down with Dax and the rogue took a toll on him. I knew this land's wards were heavy as fuck, so how did they get onto the property? I knew all of his questions and fears that his Pack once again was under attack.

"The wards you have around your property are fine. But I believe they may not go deep enough into the earth. LaToya and I will fix the issue once this shit is contained.

"Are you saying it isn't over?" Devana asked. I looked at her, but she was eyeing Blossom with some slight hesitation. Blossom stood up to her full height and dusted herself off before meeting Devana's eyes.

"It will not be over until the Enchanter is found and killed," Blossom stated.

"You know a lot about these things, demon," Devana growled. I moved swiftly, catching Dax's arm before he could connect with me. I knew what it was and why his instinct to protect his Mate would surface. I squeezed enough to snap him out of his haze of protectiveness. I didn't want a scene, and we did not have time for one. I also did not want others to see this and think there was a problem.

"Dax, are you in control?" I growled low. I knew the red ring in my eyes glowed deeper as I kept eye contact with him until he got the point. His arm shook with so much force I knew he was fighting his need to dominate. They were still newly Mated, and I understood, but I was Alpha over all of them. "Get control of it," I grunted. I held the eyes of the taller man until he looked down and away.

"I have it," he growled. "My bad. I..."

"No need for all of that. I knew you would react like that and why. I also know that when an Alpha is new, they feel the need to challenge, and I wanted to dead that shit right now.

It's natural, Devana, but we don't have time. Now, I know what you are and that you are a Hunter. But when I bring someone with me, consider them as part of my Pack unless I say otherwise. Yes, she is a demon, but she is loyal to one person, Taria Cross. That means she is loyal to anyone attached to her Queen. Do you understand where I am coming from, or should I waste time explaining it further?" I asked as I dropped Dax's arm. Devana's eyes were wide and her mouth opened.

"Stay dead!" Shani shouted. I looked back and saw she was stomping the Cicada in the chest until it stopped moving. She was breathing heavily and clenching her fists. I knew it was time to push harder with her training. It was coming faster than I thought. The aggression, anger, and outbursts were just the start. Blossom moved over to Shani as I turned back to the two Alphas.

"I...I understand, Alpha. I didn't mean...I didn't know, but I should have known," Devana said.

"I get it. I really do, especially since you didn't sense anything or have a vision. You feel that urge to protect your Pack, and that's how you should feel. I can tell you it isn't over and they will come again. We need to figure out how to keep them down. Destroying the heart is the way it's done, but the problem is that they are re-growing them. Whoever is fucking doing this is powerful as hell, but so are we. The fastest way to secure this property and people is to stop that person. Speak to Journee to see if she can disrupt the magic keeping them going. I will find LaToya and end this shit," I growled. I could feel that she was further away and I had to catch up.

"We got this here. Handle what you need to, Quinn. The Pack will defend until they are all dead," Dax said. I nodded once, before looking at Blossom. I looked at Shani and then at the house where my children were.

"I will guard them with my life," she stated. "Bring them back, or my Queen will be displeased."

I nodded and took off toward my Mate. When she said them, I knew she absolutely meant to bring Damon's ass back, or she would be displeased. I don't think anyone with a brain would want to deal with a pissed-off Shade who could make copies of herself.

CHAPTER 10
SHANI

How does Hell or evil always know when to fuck up a good moment? One minute I am being told that I will become Delta of the Savir Pack, and the next, we had freaking giant ass Cicadas digging their way from the ground. My thoughts seemed to go blank at the idea of these things getting their claws on the children. I was there when Blossom and Damon told the story of what happened on Halloween. They went after the kids, and I was not about to let that happen here. I knew these pups and cubs, so that would not fly with me. I knew I had to chill when Quinn gave Blossom that look. That same look he gives Camron when he, Taria, and Toya all go out. That "watch her" look. I reined my emotions back before looking at Dax and Devana.

"I will go and find Journee," I said. I needed something to do and not be around the evil that I could feel crawling its way to the surface. Dax frowned at me slightly, and I knew he could see me shaking. I crossed my arms over my chest, and Devana looked towards Dax, then back at me. I looked at Blossom and saw the quick nod, but I knew she would be by my side if anything were to happen.

"Good idea. We need to figure this mess out while Quinn

and the others handle the one who is behind this bullshit," Devana said. I nodded once and took off toward the house. I knew Dax was trying to read me, and I saw his brows pull together when he couldn't. Quinn announced that I would be joining his Pack tonight, but it happened the night before they all went to Hell. I knew where I wanted to be and who my true family was, which validated my place in his Pack and their lives. Now I don't have to leave when I turn eighteen. I gave my loyalty and oath that night, and it would never change, no matter how much I loved everyone here. I knew none of them could control whatever was inside of me. Not like how I knew Quinn could handle it, just in case I went off the deep end. I had a lot of pent-up anger from my past and I am terrified it will all come rushing out. I was terrified that I would hurt someone that didn't deserve it. I pushed open the massive doors and came crashing into Maeze. She caught me by the arms, and it was reflex to break free from any hold. Only that shit didn't work on her, but she noticed what I wanted to do and spun me around, pushing me away.

"I apologize. I just didn't want you to open the circle," she said. Her voice was soothing. It was also matter of fact, like she knew the reason for my reaction.

"Oh, oh hell, I am so sorry. I didn't even see it. Thank you, I know that takes time and power. Do you know where I can find Journee?" I asked just as the first howl split the air. I looked back through the door and saw those damn bugs trying and failing to breach the stairs. They wanted in the house, and we all knew the reason why.

"Is there a plan? Removing the hearts is not working," Maeze growled. I could feel an ancient power rolling off of her like Blossom. The only difference was that it was more similar to what was inside of me.

"Yes and no. Journee may be able to cut through the magic that is letting them regrow their hearts. That's why they aren't staying down," I said, looking around. They must have had all the children and other shifters down in the bunkers. The warding around this house seemed more potent than before, but it only made it harder for them to get inside. If we didn't do something now, they would make it inside, which no one wanted to happen.

"She is sitting in the very center of the house in the wing where—"

"I know the spot! Thanks," I said, taking a deeper breath. The rotting smell filled my senses, but I could scent Journee underneath it. I could get a picture of her in my mind and could tell she sat in a circle with her eyes closed, surrounded by candles as Dimitri watched in a corner. I saw her son sitting opposite her, but he seemed to be withdrawn into himself. I burst through the doors, blinking fast, trying to shake the image from my mind. I had no clue how I did that, but everything was exactly how I pictured it once I entered.

"Shai? What is it?" Dimitri asked as he pushed the white of his hair back. His eyes looked me over, making sure I wasn't hurt. The fact he just realized I was in the house told me a lot. Journee shook a little before opening her dark brown eyes to look at us both.

"I'm good, Tri. I...well, Dax wants Journee to come out and see if she can trace the magic that is animating the ***Akhkhazu.*** Before Quinn left to help Toya find the one behind this, he said to get Journee," I stated. Journee stood up, brushing her pants off and blinking fast as she processed everything. I heard footsteps behind me and I turned to see Leodora with a hand full of food. Her brows were raised, and I noticed she looked down at my hand. I quickly shook it. I had no clue why or how my hand shifted on its own. "Oh, sorry," I said, turning back to Journee. I saw out of the corner of my eye that Dimitri saw what Leodora had seen, but I knew he knew what it was and that I should not have been able to do that. It was close enough to the form that an Alpha could take. It had to be the fluctuating power running through my blood as my power shifted.

"I can try. That would at least stop them from coming back, but it will not stop more from coming," Journee stated. Journee stepped over the circle and moved to her son, who seemed to snap out of whatever daze he was in, and looked at his mother. "Zaccai, I need you to go with the other children where it is safe until I get back."

"What? No, why, mom?"

"Zaccai, this is not the time for questions. I told you what I need you to do, and I expect you to do it. Now, when this is over, we can talk about everything, but right now, I need you safe,"

"Who is going to watch your back out there? Mrs. Toya is gone. We are the only magic people," he said, frowning.

"I will help your mom with the magic stuff and make sure she gets back to you safely," Dimitri said. The look that little boy gave him almost had me on the floor. All kids loved the Beta. All kids loved Tri, all except this one, apparently. I could tell that Dimitri wanted to let the kid know that his mother would be okay but wasn't sure how to speak to the boy. That was a first for the Beta.

"We don't need your help!"

"Zaccai! Cut it, now! There are bad things out there and I need to help keep you along with everyone else safe," Journee snapped. She turned to look at me and then past me. "Oh, good. Leodora, can you please take him with you to be with the other children?"

"Yes, of course," Leodora smiled.

"Zaccai, I need you to go," Journee said as the boy stood up. I could smell the tears gathered in his eyes, but none fell as he stomped past his mother. I watched as her fingers brushed over the top of his head as he followed Leodora out of the room. I wish I knew what it felt like to have a mother. I shook that thought out of my head before looking up at the two. Dimitri and Journee spoke in a language I had never heard before, when they both looked up.

"We may know a way to stop the flow of magic that keeps growing the new hearts. Let's move," Dimitri said. We all rushed out of the house and stopped at the crowd of tall, leathery-faced creatures that covered the front yard. Their beady red eyes glowed as the chittering and buzzing sound increased as more came from beneath the ground.

We stood at the top of the steps, and I had no clue where to go or what to do. The wolves were doing all they could, but it was just entirely too many of them.

"What do we need to do?" I asked, looking at the two. Dimitri cracked his neck from side to side, taking in the chaos. I could feel every hit against the barrier to the house, and I knew it would fall, and soon.

"We need to get them away from the house. At least thin it out a little, so it does not go against it. Shani, we need to attack and thin them out, but I will need you to bring a heart back inside the ward for Journee. Then come back and keep them from getting inside," Dimitri growled. I looked at him and saw that he was shifting into his giant wolf. It was still beautiful to see because his fur's black and white colors never mixed. It was different to see in a wolf, but I knew more about him than being a shifter.

"Shani, try not to damage the heart if possible. We may only have one shot at this," Journee said while drawing a circle. She settled herself in the middle and whispered words I could barely hear or understand. I didn't ask what they were up to because there was no time. We may have all the best and strongest fighters, but that meant nothing when the enemy wouldn't understand the assignment and stay the hell down! I closed my eyes, letting the shift take hold of me, and when I opened them, I felt nothing but rage. I saw the enemy in front of us, and all I could think was that they were coming for the children! They wanted the twins, to hurt everyone who cared about me. I shot off the stairs, leaping in the air and over the crowd of ***Akhkhazu.*** I landed behind them, but I wasted no time dragging one down as Dimitri dove into the ones in front. I knew what needed to be done instinctively.

We had to hit the front and back to get their numbers down. Not just for that, but also to stop others from joining in from behind. I tore through them all, ripping bodies apart, only thinking about keeping all I loved safe. I howled when a claw attached to my back leg and pulled. One of the bugs was digging beneath us, and that was when I noticed the stone steps. They were cracking, and I saw the clawed hands of many ***Akhkhazu*** breaking through the barrier. That is when I remembered what I was supposed to do as everything snapped back into focus. I twisted, but being in this form, that thing would pull me under in no time. I felt a power inside of me that screamed anger, darkness, and calculating. I never wanted to focus too much on it because it felt like I turned into someone else or something else. I let all thoughts leave my mind and reached for that darkness inside me. I barely touched it when everything went black, then a burst of gold-filled my vision as I moved through the crowd. I was on two legs and no longer a wolf. I felt like a ghost as I moved and knew something was up when I passed by Dimitri, and he didn't seem to notice me. I grabbed an ***Akhkhazu*** and dug myself into dried skin. I shoved my entire arm inside of it and felt my hand wrap around a cold lump of flesh. I knew what I was touching and it almost made me sick. I yanked it out and held it in one hand while taking the body in the other and throwing it hard enough to make a gap to the first step. I moved faster, leaping up the stairs, and dropped the heart in front of Journee, who screamed. She looked around before looking down, seeing the yellowish-green beating heart in front of her.

"Sha—Shani? Where..."

"No time! Stop them!" I growled, but it sounded more like an echo from miles away. I did see Journee jump slightly, but I turned to face the new crowd of ***Akhkhazu*** clawing their way from beneath the stone. I felt that power drop at that moment, leaving me standing there naked and panting. My arms were covered in the green insides of the bugs, but I knew it wasn't over. I took in a breath, realizing that I would have to fight hand to hand when I felt a presence beside me. I looked over at the woman as her eyes glowed lavender and another woman with teal-tipped hair.

"I guess there is no time like the present to start some of your training. The first thing to learn is never to think that you will fight alone when you have a Pack behind you," Maeze growled. Then she flashed forward with a speed I only ever felt once and was just a few seconds ago.

"You have an ancient power in you, child. I think I will assist the Gamma in your training as well," the teal-eyed woman said. I turned to look at her and damn near screamed myself as her head shifted and her mouth grew wider and wider. "Now, show us your skills," she said and followed after Maeze. I didn't know who they were, but I really wanted to know why Quinn would choose them to train me when I was just a Delta?

Chapter 11
Latoya

Damon followed closely behind me as we moved through the surrounding wooded area of the Rayne property. I was moving faster than a human, but I could go faster. I knew if I tapped into Quinn's power, I would, but I didn't want to take from him while he dealt with those giant ass Cicadas.

We are dead.

But we live.

We are dead, but we live.

Again and again.

The whispers started to be more forceful than they had been before. I didn't know if Damon could tell the strain of not giving in to those voices was affecting me. They were lost and needed help, but that is what it appeared to be. I could feel the underlying evilness to the voices, but I couldn't figure out why or what they were at this point. I knew they weren't the usual whispers that spoke to me every day, and it seemed like these newer voices pushed the others back. I could sense the magic, and the further we went, the stronger it seemed to get. I knew they were not on this property directly, but close enough for me to sense them. I caught Damon looking up to the sky with a frown. Then he noticed I was watching his crazy ass. Damon sucked his fang and raised a perfect brow as if I didn't know what the hell I was doing. He is such an asshole! Just looking at him gets on my nerves.

"Do you know where the hell you are going, or are you just running around the forest like a Keebler elf?" He asked once we slowed down. I knew he could feel my intense anger rolling off of me in waves, but I didn't know if he knew the whispers were louder than ever before. I couldn't help but roll my eyes at him before flicking my gaze to his, only to see a yellow ball of energy coming toward us.

"Move!" I said, jumping in front of him and holding up my hands. The markings along my arms began to climb up to my collarbone as I caught the energy with my own power. I infused it with my power by pushing heat into the ball, turning it from yellow to a burning blue and white flame. I raised my arms, then pulled my hands, sending the power in two directions. The magic came from that direction, but I could feel whoever sent it was on the move.

"I guess we are going in the right direction. Thanks, itty-bitty. Now, which way?"

"They will not be in the direction where that shit came from, so we follow the other flame I threw back," I panted. I felt that I was working harder than I should, but I knew it was because my brain was fighting a mental assault. The whispers wouldn't stop, and they repeated those four phrases non-stop!

"Toya!"

"What!" I snapped my hand to the side and I heard myself growl. I cleared my throat and placed my hand to my eyes, rubbing them. "What?" I tried again. Damon narrowed his eyes but said nothing. His fangs were peeking out as he approached me, but then he flashed forward. I was flung over his shoulder as we began to follow after the flame I threw. I knew that it would follow the Witch until it caught them.

"What the fuck! I knew you would slip and try to kidnap me again. You have a serious fixation with me!" I screamed. The deep chuckle caught me by surprise, making me almost laugh.

"Lesson number two is you are what you were born to be. You are what you are meant to be. You just need to accept it and bend it to your will," Damon said. I narrowed my eyes because I didn't know what I was meant to be. How can I know when I didn't fully know myself? I had no clue who my father was until that whole shit with Taria.

"Make it make sense, because how am I supposed to be what I was born to be if I don't know exactly who I am?"

"Just because it's lesson number two doesn't mean you will figure it out now. Lesson two is designed to make you think. You are letting voices that should be dead and gone mess with you. Own up to what you are so that you can control it," he said, and then he went motionless. Damon dropped me to the ground on my feet, and I felt his large hands spinning in the direction of the flame. I noticed that the voices weren't so loud as before, but all that shit went out the window when I saw a figure stand up. He was wearing what looked like a black cloak with a hood covering most of his face. He was tall with broad shoulders, and he held my flame back with one hand.

"A Warlock," I gritted.

"He is powerful. Maybe as powerful as you are," Damon growled. Damon raised his head and sniffed before a low guttural growl left his mouth. He didn't need to say anything because I already knew what was up. I already knew what these voices were and why they were here.

"Necromancer."

"He might be powerful, but he damn sure ain't got nothing on me!" I made sure my statement was loud enough for the Warlock to hear. The man raised his head as flashing yellowish-green eyes stared back at me and laughed. This man wasn't just a Warlock. He was becoming something much worse. I knew Damon was fucking with me, but I also knew exactly how crazy a Necromancer could be once they align themselves with a demon. This fool was getting a boost of power from somewhere and I would find out who to destroy them.

“Your power means nothing compared to what I hold, Grey Witch,” he laughed. I could hear the slight accent of something I had heard once before. The thought brought me back to when Quinn and I went to fucking Florida.

“Necromancy? Since you can do a little parlor trick, you believe that you got something on me?” I knew I was talking shit as we moved closer. I could sense the wards around the property and knew they were also guarded against demons. The solid black marks crawled over his hands and arms, showing hints of pale skin. The hood finally fell back and my eyes widened because I knew exactly who he was and why he was here.

“Gregory Beaumont, I’d hoped you wouldn’t come here seeking revenge, but I see that I was wrong. And I see that you are just that stupid,” I said, standing next to the burning flame. I watched as he closed his hand, extinguishing the fire as if it were nothing. I raised a brow as I took him in and realized quickly that something was off.

“So you know me. So what? Do you think I care what happens to these dogs? I am here to finish what Valerie couldn’t do.”

“Honestly, I could give a shit what you think or what you feel like you came here to do. I only care about ripping out your heart,” I spat.

“If that’s all you got with this bullshit flame, I am disappointed. Step over the line Toya or I will send—”

“Fuck this monologue bullshit!” Damon growled and launched himself over the line. His fist came down just as Gregory managed to get a hand up. I wanted to say something, but I was legit about to do the same thing, so I joined Damon.

Gregory used his power and knocked Damon away before the punch could connect.

"Oh, and I think you forgot about the other flame," I said as I threw both arms down. The second flame I threw came back around and slammed into Gregory, driving his body to the ground. I let the fire inside of me out, and as it covered my body, I moved. Damon was already over Gregory, punching him repeatedly in the chest. A strong force of power exploded, blowing us both away. Damon slammed hard into a tree, cracking it into pieces. I slammed into a muscular chest and felt Quinn's arms wrap around me before we hit the ground. I looked up and saw the red of his eyes glow when a sudden pressure seemed to weigh heavy on my body and mind.

"None of you understand power! None of you know what it is like to be chosen by the Goddess. I am no Necromancer, nor am I just a Warlock! I control the dead, and I can bring them back to life as many times as needed."

I pushed through the mental wave of power when I felt Quinn's hand on my shoulder. Our mental strength together was harder to tear down. I stepped forward using our combined power and pushed through the mental shield Gregory had placed around himself. I raised a hand and spread my fingers wide, then closed them tightly, effectively cutting off the air in his bubble of space.

"*Infernal.* So you traded your birth-given magic to play with dead bodies? You may be a more powerful Necromancer, but you still need to breathe," I gritted. I could see him through the blue-green of my sight, but I could tell something wasn't right. This was too easy. I saw Damon moving out of the corner of my eye, making me release the grip I had on the air surrounding Gregory.

"Bitch!" Gregory gritted, sucking in a breath. But he managed to block Damon's kick, but he missed the green blast that came from his fist when he twisted out of his grip. The blast sent Gregory flying across the ground.

"Damon, what the fuck are you doing?" Quinn grunted as we ran toward the fight.

"You fucking bastard! Where are you? Let go of this soul! Let it go!" Damon growled as he slammed his fist so fast into Gregory's face. I couldn't see in between each contact he made because they were so fast.

"I knew one of you would recognize this face. I thought it would be the Witch, but—" Gregory coughed. I blinked and then held out my hand to stop Quinn from getting any closer. I knew something was off. I could see it now. With each hit, the face began to shift. His pale skin now became leathery brown with facial features that seemed almost familiar. His teeth became more needle-like while his eyes turned a burning red, just like the ***Akhkhazu***. I knew this wasn't Gregory Beaumont but was just another one of his puppets. So if the Infernal Nercrolock wasn't here, where is he, and who is that? Why did I know this face, but it seemed *older*? I sucked in a breath as I realized why the face looked so familiar.

"No, no! What the hell?" I whispered. Then I was just as pissed as Damon, but I had a feeling it was for a different reason. Damon slammed his fist into the chest and ripped out the heart.

"You should have never used this body or captured this soul," Damon growled. I moved closer with Quinn beside me when I heard his low growl behind me. I froze because it was one I had never heard come from him since we had been together. Before doing anything, Quinn moved and had Damon by the wrist before inhaling deeply. His usual black and red-ringed eyes seemed to bleed into full black as a pinprick of red shone through like a laser beam. He figured it out, and I knew things had worsened for my Alpha. This Warlock hadn't just gone after dead bodies who were evil in life or captured only evil souls. He deliberately chose one that would deal the most emotional harm to every one of us. I just couldn't figure out how that was until I realized how personal this attack was, and it was because of me. It was my name that they were attacking and the one bitch who knew my history better than anyone, was my Aunt Ellen. She was the true darkness behind Valerie, giving her strength. She was also the dark presence that nearly killed my children and me before Garrett showed up to help me. So, they used Garrett's father in the bullshit game they were playing.

"You think you can use my Wolves? You will regret ever thinking of using any past or present wolf as one of your puppets," Quinn growled. I felt my tears and anger boil over at this point because that bitch thought she could use Tucker Jackson, a wolf, and Garrett's father, in this twisted fucking game!

I live and die.

I need to die.

I need to be free.

The whisper cut through all the rest, and I knew exactly who it was speaking to. I could hear Tucker's words, the pain, anger, and anguish.

"Toya! I am connected to all of them! I need your power to connect with mine to stop them from coming back! Now! I need it now!"

I could hear Journee's voice loud and clear in my mind. I didn't think as I let my flames consume my body and screamed. I could see Quinn's body go stiff as I pulled on our bond and sent a massive amount of power into the air as we connected with Journee. I saw everything that was happening as if I were looking through her eyes. The property was crawling with those fucking bugs, but every last one of them stood still once I wrapped our combined power around them. I searched and searched for the source of power that controlled them. I finally was able to see the glowing form outlined in crimson on the far side of the property and knew it was him. That was the real Gregory Beaumont, and I would burn his ass alive. I would show his soul what torture actually was for fucking with my family. Then the next one is that Witch Ellen Grey and whoever the fuck else gets in my way!

~

Deadly Secrets

Once I opened my eyes, I could tell that all of those damn Cicadas were down. We had broken the repeater spell, but that didn't stop the Warlock. I looked at Quinn, then Damon, as the heart turned to dust. I looked down, and the husk beneath Damon turned to ashes. So, it was twofold because that heart didn't belong to Tucker, but it was his body.

"He isn't free! I can still hear him in my head," Damon grunted. I had no time to drill his ass about how he could hear Tucker in his mind. We had to get back to the others, and we needed to kill that bitch ass Warlock before he got away. Damon is correct because I knew for a fact that the other souls wanted this, but he did not, and his soul screamed to be released.

"I know. We will get him to where he should be," I said. I looked at Quinn as he stared in the direction of the house. "Let's get back now before he gets too far away. I will have Journee start on a spell so something like this can never happen again," I said. I heard Damon growl, but he was already gone.

"Can you tell if he is moving and which way he is going?" Quinn asked. I closed my eyes just as I felt Quinn's shift flowing over him.

"He's moving east! We need to go before he uses a portal," I shouted. I opened my eyes and climbed on Quinn's back as he took off toward the Necrolock. The thoughts that ran through my mind played havoc with my emotions. How had he gotten to Garrett's father, and why? I felt Quinn's thoughts shift toward mine.

"Did Garrett ever tell you what Pack attacked when his parents were killed?"

"No. Garrett doesn't really talk about it, and when he does, it's only a little information here and there."

"I will ask Dax. It couldn't have been that long ago when it happened, but I want to know why. What was the reason for the attack?"

I sat up when I felt the sudden shift in magic, and the whispers from Tucker became more insistent and pained.

I live and die.

I need to die.

I need to be free.

I live and die.

I need to die.

I need to be free.

Save, save, save.

I felt the pull of magic and knew what was about to happen. He held hundreds of souls and could bring back any number of them, so why this one? If he had it the entire time, why did he take it and keep it? I didn't sense any other souls like him, so I knew he didn't have Garrett's mother's soul or Lily's parents. Something just was not adding up and I did not like that shit one bit. Once I get the answers I need, everybody will pay for all this has caused.

I saw the portal ahead of us and I could tell he had already passed through it. I would be right behind his ass because I knew who was pulling the strings! All of this shit was a setup, but how long back had it gone? How would Ellen know I would end up with these shifters or hell being a part of the supernatural world? The portal grew smaller the closer we got, so I reached out with my own magic, trying and failing to hold it open. The whispers of the others became louder, making it harder to concentrate on the location. "He's working with that bitch Ellen!"

"How do you know?"

"Beaumont! That old lady with the creepy twins in New Orleans is a Beaumont. She knew who I was and she told us to go on our date. The woman at the counter knew what I was and then the Druids showed up! Then, once we had the babies, the bitch came for them! Her dirty fingers are all in this pot and I can feel her magic in waves. That bitch has been setting us up from jump, and now taking it to new levels, by attacking our people!"

The portal snapped shut just like I knew it would, but I had an idea where the bastard was heading. Funny enough is that we would be going in the same fucking direction. Whispers faded from my sheer force of *Will.* I was so tired of the betrayals and secrets coming from every direction. I got that everything was about power and I knew for a fact Ellen wanted what was mine. It just made little sense as to how Garrett's father had anything to do with it. I turned to Quinn once he shifted and saw anger written across his face that I had never seen before.

"No matter if a wolf is dead or alive, they belong to me, LaToya. When we get to that fake Warlock, his life is mine for thinking he had the right to use Tucker's body this way. I love you, but do not get in my way on this one," he growled. I probably would have taken a step back, but I knew that Quinn would never hurt me. I knew she would have said he was turning me on if Taria was here, and her ass would be absolutely correct. I also understood exactly where he was coming from due to the bond of being Twice Marked. "Why the fuck would they use Garrett's father?"

"She saw Garrett that day when he came to help the twins and me. She knows he is like family to me," I sighed. I pulled back the fire threatening to consume my blood and body. I was pissed as fuck, but I knew I had to chill out. I had to calm down so I could think clearly.

"I feel you, babe, but he has held that soul since Tucker's death. I couldn't scent Tucker, but I could feel deep inside that he was a wolf. He belongs to the Alpha. He should have taken his place with ***Kannuck***,"

"Yes, yes, he should, and he will, baby. I promise you that much," I said.

"I know it will happen, but we are missing something," Quinn stated.

"Yeah, a hell of a lot, but we need to get back. That Warlock, Necromancer, Necrolock isn't dead, so those things could still reappear. It may just take longer," I said, pacing.

"I doubt they will, but we should make sure it never has the chance again. We should leave once you and Journee ward this place from top to bottom. They want us panicked and divided. They didn't know we were heading their way, so we need to figure out how they knew we were here," Quinn said. I clamped my mouth shut because I wanted to scream. Dax's Pack didn't need any more bullshit happening, and it was as if we brought it right to their doorstep. Quinn was right, we had to leave. We needed to deal with these Circles sooner rather than later. Then I will kill that bitch Ellen and take out whoever followed her along this death path!

12 CHAPTER DAMON

I made it back to the house and saw Blossom cleaning off her swords. I scanned the area, looking for Dax to figure out what the fuck happened and how? I might have been losing my mind when I smelled that scent, but I knew damn well I was not going crazy. From what Garrett spoke about his parents, it was minimal when it came to their background. I knew he had shown me some things in the books that he reads, which seemed impossible, but I knew that the kid was special. The books basically only said that Garrett is a part of two strong bloodlines. The Grey and Cross bloodline lived in that kid, giving him gifts beyond what a normal werewolf would have. The Cross blood meant that he could read the words on the page and only tell me about them because I couldn't understand them. I have had Taria's blood, but not enough that I could read a book or scroll only meant for a Cross. Garrett belonged with Taria and Toya just as much as their biological children, but what caught me off guard more was my scent. He carried the scent of my blood. Only one Pack and one shifter I knew should hold my scent, and his name was not Tucker Jackson. His name was Taj Jabari. I considered

Taj as my family more than a friend because of our Blood Bond we created together as children. I never understood what exactly happened to him or his family.

One moment they were there, and the next, they were long gone, but that was so long ago before Michael was born. How in the fuck could Taj actually be Garrett's father? I shook my head as memories and thoughts flowed back into my mind. Some I wanted, but it was a hell of a lot more I did not want to see.

"Damon. What happened? Is it dead?" Blossom asked. Her hand gripped my forearm, and I reflexively yanked it away. I took a deep breath as she frowned at me. Blossom crossed her arms over her chest and raised a brow. "What the hell is your problem? You look as if you saw a ghost?" She smirked. I knew she was fucking with me because she knew damn well that I could not only see them, but they got on my last nerve. At least they stayed far away from me since my trip back from Hell.

"No! No, he isn't dead, nor is he a regular Warlock. He's– he is something else altogether and did something that he will regret once I rip out every organ from his body," I growled. I felt my fangs slip past my lips and the second set was not far behind. I needed answers, but if anything, Dax and the brothers should have known another Royal shifter when they saw one.

"We will kill him, Damon. Whatever happened, it will be taken care of, and you know that, so what else is happening? You look like the demon Toya accuses you of being right now," Blossom asked again. This time, when her hand touched me, I didn't move. I let her scent and energy wash over me, seemingly calming everything inside my mind. I swallowed hard, pulling back my anger so that I could think straight.

"I need answers and the first person to start with would be Dax. After that, we should get the hell out of here and take the bitch down," I said. I started for the main house as other Pack members filtered out throughout the property.

"You still haven't said what is on your mind. Do not make me ask again," Blossom stated. She may have sounded like a joke or tried to be stern to everyone else, but I knew better. I knew full well that she might get in her head to stick those shadowy fingers in my brain and pull it out. I knew it would be a battle of the mind, but it wasn't needed this time, and I didn't want her to know what I had been up to at the moment.

"No need, Shade. The Warlock Gregory used a dead werewolf's body by the name of Tucker Jackson as a puppet," I said, stopping in front of the stone stairs. I turned to face Blossom and stared into blue, orange, green, and pink eyes that swirled and mixed as she blinked. I saw the frown and then the anger on her face.

"That is the name of Garrett's father. What the fuck!"

"Exactly! That is bad enough, but it gets worse, but I want to tell this shit once," I said. I looked to the north and could smell Toya and Quinn as they approached.

"Yes, yes, I understand. Let's find the Alphas and figure this out. What Gregory has done will not go unpunished. I have a perfect space in a dimension to torture such *Beings*," Blossom said as she took two stairs at a time. I turned around, following her, wondering what kind of shit she was doing when not around us. Who the fuck has a pocket dimension for torture? Now, thanks to Blossom, I want one for myself. We stepped through the doors, and the first people I spotted were Dimitri and Devana. I looked around quickly, but I didn't see Dax anywhere. I wasn't worried because I knew where his Mate would be. He wasn't far away. Dimitri spotted us and started in our direction as wolves, bears, and other shifters moved around, cleaning up the house.

"Damon! What happened? Did we get the bastard?"

"No. We will, though. Don't worry about that. I can tell you we will be leaving soon, but I have questions. Where the fuck is your Alpha?" I couldn't help the growl that escaped, and honestly, I didn't give a shit.

"You need to chill the fuck out, Damon. Tensions are still high. I get it, but show some fucking respect!" Dimitri grunted.

"You think I give a fuck about respect for the shit I just saw? Something that should have never fucking occurred! I don't give a fuck who is and who ain't an Alpha! So, sit your Beta ass down," I gritted.

"Damon! This is unnecessary. They are not who you are angry with, and you are letting your anger control you," Blossom said. In a flash, she was on me, and I felt her around me. It was as if she was inside of me, pulling me back. Having to feel is bullshit and feeling these emotions now when I felt nothing for years seems way too fucking much.

"Step away from my Beta. Listen to your pet demon over there and back the fuck up," Devana snapped. I could tell Blossom's words registered with Dimitri and he knew something was off. He and I never had a problem, so we knew when something wasn't right.

"The fuck is happening?" Dax's bass voice vibrated the room, and Dimitri took a deliberate step back, but I kept my eyes on the new Luna of the Pack.

"I think you need to get a handle on your Bitch," I smirked. I needed to release this anger and fighting was the way to go.

"Who the fuck do you think you are?"

"So you mean you not a Bitch? Dax, get your Mate cause this Bitch is trippin if she thinks slick remarks about demons will fly around here," I said. I felt Dax coming, and I ducked low and came up with a green energy ball when I heard the click of heels.

"If I have to make every last one of you fall and bare your

neck, I will. Now stop with the bullshit and sit the fuck down!" Quinn boomed through the entire house. I sucked my teeth because that command shit wouldn't work with me and Dax seemed like the perfect one to go one-on-one with. At least I knew the fight would last long.

"Damon, stop with the shit before I call Katherine," Toya said. I flicked my eyes over to her and saw the short little asshole had her phone out.

"Well played, mini-me, well played," I said, letting the glowing ball fade. Toya came into the room and went straight up to Devana. Before looking at Dax, she looked up, cocking her head to the side.

"I like you, Dax, and love your Pack as if they are my family, but you need to teach this one. I know damn well my husband, your True Alpha, has expressed his thoughts about OUR demon. If you, Hunter, can't get with the program, better training will be needed. I will speak to Taria on this, and she will rectify the situation, because Blossom is her Shade. A lot of shit just happened, and I want to make sure it doesn't happen again. I will check on my babies, then Journee, and I will make sure this can never happen again," Toya stated before walking off toward the twins. I looked at Quinn and saw the same rage I felt, but I knew it was from the desecration of the body of his wolf. Dimitri stepped forward in the silence, still watching me. He stood next to Dax, who looked as if he just got control enough not to take my bait, and that sucked.

"My Beta has filled me in that you have questions. What the hell do you need to know during all of this shit we got going on," Dax gritted. I smiled and looked at Blossom, who looked bored.

"How did you not know that Tucker Jackson was Taj Jabari?" I laid that question down and everyone near us went utterly silent.

"What?"

"Taj Jabari."

"That...that is impossible. I would have known it was him and you know that! You got to be mistaken," Dax said, confused.

"Jabari? Like Kya Jabari? That family was taken hostage over eighteen or nineteen years ago and is now freed because of Kya. A lot of their people and Royal family members were killed during that time," Quinn stated.

"Kya is a Jabari? I thought her name was Naazeer?"

"Yes, after she and Kahlil got married, but she is of Pack Jabari," Quinn stated matter-of-factly. I turned back to Dax, and he looked shocked.

"What did he look like to you? No, wait, tell me what Garrett looks like to you."

"What?"

"Just humor me," I said, looking back at Quinn.

"Smart kid. Short, brown skin, and skinny with a low cut. I mean, he just looked like a normal little pup. Nothing really stood out," Dax said.

"What about Lily?"

"Pretty like thing. Always laughing and is a sweet girl. She had large hazel eyes with little freckles across her face and long, straight black hair," Dax said. I cocked my head to the side, studying him before looking at Quinn, who had the same 'what the fuck' look on his face.

"I do not understand what you are getting at, Damon. You come in here starting shit after we just finished dealing with a bunch of bullshit while you were nowhere to be found," Devana said. I could tell she was picking up on her Mates' sudden confusion and the pain that seemed to make his brow furrow. I flicked my eyes at Dimitri and saw the same thing.

"What did Tucker look like to you?"

"Tall swimmers build dark brown skin. He looked like a normal person, and his wolf wasn't anything spectacular," Dax grunted. I watched as he spoke, and the pain eased on his face, but I saw whatever spell Taj had on Dax and others had snapped right at that moment. "What the fuck!"

"No, no hell no, that...that should be impossible!" Dimitri suddenly growled.

"What? What the hell is going on here?" Devana asked. I stepped closer and placed a hand on Dax, who looked at me sharply.

"I didn't see it. Damon, I did not see it! You know I would have sent them somewhere else for safety. They were here for, for years! I mean years and Garrett...what the hell! I swear he seemed to age slowly and I never once thought about it. I just knew I had to care for him and Lily. That's all I had to do until it was time. He is a Jabari, not Jackson, but I know a Tucker Jackson out there, and he has a son. Somehow, it's all just been taken from my mind," Dax stated. I looked at Dimitri when his back hit the wall at the knowledge. I looked back to see Quinn staring up at the ceiling, not moving, talking, or breathing. I know what Garrett told me. What he read in those books had to be true. The story wasn't about his parents but another wolf shifter with Cross DNA. I let Dax go and stepped back so his Mate could get closer. I may be closer with Malic, but I knew that Dax knew that Taj and I were brothers bonded by blood.

I felt Blossom come up to my side, and I wanted to get closer to her. I felt she could shield me from the pain I knew was coming when I processed all this shit. I felt her hand slip into mine, which made me glance up. Her brows were bunched together in thought and I knew she picked up on something none of us had been thinking.

"Has anyone stopped to think what all this means? The Warlock has the soul of a powerful wolf-shifter that had Cross blood once running through his veins. I know Garrett has Grey blood running through him as well, making him powerful. There is nothing like the True Alpha, but he would be great when it is time for him to be because of his level of power now. His mother had to be a powerful Witch for a spell-like this and I bet she was the Grey Witch. Probably one who got away just like Toya's mother escaped," Blossom stated. I just nodded because she was right and that was going to be some crazy shit once we got home. "Also, if you are right about the real Tucker Jackson, then he may not be dead, and neither is his son. Does anyone know what a demon would give to have someone with even a little Cross blood inside them? How they could use their blood if they give in to the torture?" My thought process was so fucked up I didn't even hear the clicking of Toya's heels.

"I know you are fucking lying. Ain't no fucking way this shit has happened and none of us knew a fucking thing," she sighed.

"Shouldn't the demon know who is fucking with Hunter blood?" Devana asked. I could tell she wasn't being a Bitch this time and genuinely wanted to know, but I also knew Toya was at her limit. She was too short for this ride and I moved to snatch her ass back before going to the Luna.

"That's like saying we all look-alike or some shit! What the—"

"LaToya!" Quinn snapped and I let her short ass go. Her feet did not hit the floor because Quinn scooped her up before she could go off again.

"Fuck that, Quinn! I should let Damon fuck some shit up in this bitc—"

"Hey! So you all will tell me that no one noticed that I have been missing this entire time? Not one person is going to ask about that big ass owl?" Malic said, panting. I looked back at the door and saw a dirty ass Malic standing there with leaves, sticks, and dirt all over his clothes.

"We noticed your ass went and hid from the bugs, is what we noticed," Dimitri said with his arms crossed. I bit down on my tongue, not saying shit. Malic growled as he brushed off his clothes.

"Fuck you, Dee! Damon! You saw me, bro! You looked up and saw me because you fucking waved at me!"

"Malic, it's all good. We all know how you feel about insects," I shrugged.

"Dax!" Malic looked at his brother, who still seemed to receive information blocked from him.

"Malic, I don't have time for your crazy ass stories right now. We need to get this place cleaned up," Dax ordered before turning and leaving.

"Quinn? Come on, we were together," Malic pleaded.

"There were a lot of things happening, but if you say that's what happened then..."

"Ahh, what the fuck! This is the bullshit I be talking about!"

"Malic, come on and talk to me about it. I have heard none of the stories and I want to know," Devana said, leading Malic away. He shoulder-checked me, and I let it slide because I did see the giant ass owl, but it wasn't my place to speak about it.

"LaToya, get the twins and let's go. We need to get out of here and on the move. Are the wards in place so this cannot happen again?"

"Yeah! The fuck you think I was..."

"Check yourself. Blossom, can you find Shani and get the truck ready to move while I give the orders I need to be followed? We need to go," Quinn said before following after Dax. Blossom left the room silently, leaving Toya and me after Dimitri followed behind Quinn.

"He better check himself," Toya muttered. I laughed, and she gave me a death glare that didn't do shit. It looked like a frowning baby head.

"You know he heard that."

"I don't give a flying fuck what he heard, and why do you care?"

Toya was redlining, and I was here for the shit!

"Shut the hell up, and let's go get my little creatures from lock-up. They probably set fire to someone else's shoes," I chuckled. I felt the heat coming at my back, but what surprised me was the laugh following it.

Once everything died down, I didn't wait around for anyone to ask me what I did. I had no clue what the hell was going on with me, but I knew it was not typical of our kind. It definitely was not normal for a regular shifter like me. Quinn announced what I was to everyone and that I would be his Delta. I wasn't expecting that, but it was still an honor to be the Delta of the True Alpha. So where in the hell did all that disappearing and reappearing stuff come from back there? I was inside the RV before I knew it and digging through my bags when I heard the door open and close. I didn't need to breathe deeply to know it was Blossom, and she probably was coming to check on the teen wolf who couldn't control herself.

"I am not checking on you," Blossom called out. I finished cleaning myself up and got dressed. I pulled on my high-waisted navy-blue sports leggings and the matching navy-blue crisscross sports top. I was on the second level, so I leaned over to see her staring straight up at me.

"Seriously," I laughed. Blossom's form of being subtle meant none at all. So I should have known that what she said was exactly what she meant. She was not worried because if she were, then she would have been there when I needed her to be.

"Honestly, I wasn't worried because you did so well out there under pressure. I wanted to know how you managed to slip into the shadows. It wasn't fully and not quite how a Shade would do it, but it was close," she asked. My eyes widened and she cocked her head to the side. "You didn't know that you could do something like that?"

"Hell no!" I said, leaning back. After grabbing my hoodie, I pulled on my white Nikes and joined her on the main level.

"Mmm, I may need to speak with Quinn about a little extra training. I am not sure what it will be once you fully come into your gifts, but it's best to train with the *Beings* who are living shadows."

I opened my mouth but shut it when she abruptly turned and moved for the door.

"Wait! What is happening now? Did they kill it?" I asked, following close behind. We stepped out of the RV into what looked like organized chaos, and I spotted the two women that made my bones ache.

"No, but we will. Once Toya and the others finish up, we will leave asap to take care of this mess once and for all." I looked at Blossom as the other women moved through the shifters to where we stood. I had never heard Blossom show emotion, but I heard the anger in her voice when it hit a growl lower than my wolf's.

"Well, I will make sure we are all set to get out of here once they arrive. I should get things ready for the twins, so Toya doesn't have to stress about it," I murmured.

"No. I will do that while you speak with them about the other training you will need," Blossom said, facing me. Her eyes weren't the swirl of colors they usually were, but a deep red that had me moving out of her way. Whatever happened when Quinn, Toya, and Damon came back must be affecting her significantly. I hoped no one was hurt, but even if they weren't, whoever did what they did to piss that Shade off would not live long enough to regret it.

"Shani, you ran off before we could speak with you," Maeze said. She smiled at me as if she knew me. I knew damn well she did not and neither did this other chick. Either way, Quinn already decreed that Maeze would be training me. I also found out that I was related to her paternal side. Thank God and ***Kannuck*** for that because if it had anything to do with my mother's side of the family, I would have had to disappoint Quinn.

"Yes, you did, and I wanted to tell you how well your fight form was, even when you were naked," Remi grinned. I laughed while looking around as everyone picked up the pieces after the battle.

"Thanks, I guess. We are shifters, so we are naked for at least forty percent of our lives. Well, most of us," I shook my head. I knew many older were-shifters could have their clothes just appear back on like magic. I knew it came with age, experience, and power. I would master that technique if that shit killed me. Maeze and Remi sounded alike and not at the same time. They both had accents I could not place, and I heard many accents living at the school.

"How are we related exactly? I know we should be talking about training, but—"

"But you want to know about your father?" Maeze said, crossing her arms.

"Well, that is my queue to let you all talk. I just wanted to let you know that you did well for such a young shifter. We will speak again soon, yes?" Remi smiled. I was pretty sure I saw way too many damn teeth in her mouth.

"Thank you. Yeah, it seems that way," I said, waving as she left to help out. I turned back and saw Maeze smiling softly as she looked me over.

"I remember when your father was born. He was a handful back then, but I only saw him up until he was about four or five. You have his eyes," she said. I had no clue why I felt uncomfortable talking about my father because I loved him. Maybe it wasn't so uncomfortable, but why did no one come for him or me back then? If we had family, where in the hell were they when all of that shit went down? I shook my head, clearing those thoughts, when I heard Toya's voice. I looked up and saw her and Damon arguing again.

"So, are we like cousins or something like that?"

"Oh no, I was your father's Aunt." She laughed. Both my brows went up at that because he never said a word about family except that they were dead. "Well, great, great, great, great Aunt, but that is beside the point. I am your Aunt as well, and if I knew what the state of the Wolf Nation was, I would have come back long ago, but I was lost," she stated. I frowned as she seemed to look off into the distance. She looked regretful, and I realized how many greats she added before Aunt. I realized that my father may have thought we had no more family because he believed that she was dead with the rest of them. Then it hit me exactly how old my father had to be and how he took on an Alpha long enough for me to escape.

"I can say that it will be nice to get to know you while we train. I only had my father so—"

"Shani! Please get your children!" I looked over at Toya and saw Riaan straining to get out of her arms and Reign slapping Damon in the face.

"I think that will be nice, but don't think I will take it easy on you cause we are family," Maeze said, touching my shoulder. "Go get your children," she laughed before turning away and melting into the Pack surrounding us. I swallowed as I tried putting memories of my father and what happened that night out of my mind and moved to get the terrible two before Toya put a spell on them. Again.

"Reign, stop hitting your Uncle. Come here, little boy," I said, taking Riaan from Toya. I could tell some messed-up shit went down that Blossom didn't want to mention by the look on Toya's face.

"Thanks. Once Quinn gets his punk ass out here, we are leaving. I want to get this shit done like yesterday," Toya said. She kissed the twins and went straight for the RV. Reign stopped hitting Damon and had her arms out for me to take her as well.

"Did you see a huge Owl be chance?" Damon asked.

"Actually, I did. It was attacking those dang Cicadas," I smirked. I cocked my head to the side and raised my brows at him cause I wanted to know why he asked. I thought I was trippin at first, but at least I knew I wasn't now since he asked.

"Do me a favor and act like you didn't if anyone asks you about it. Especially if it's Malic," Damon chuckled and moved to follow his nemesis in the RV. I opened my mouth to ask Damon why, but I saw Quinn approaching us. The red ring in his eyes glowed so brightly that it was almost like a spotlight shining on us. His hands were more prominent than usual, and his black-tipped claws almost gleamed like black ice.

"Time to go, Shani."

I was not about to question him about what went down while he was like this, and I knew for Quinn to be this pissed off, everybody was about to die.

Deadly Secrets

Quinn was already in the RV, telling Damon that he would be driving this time as I helped Reign and Riaan into the vehicle. They both wanted to climb the steps, and most times, it was easier to let them do it themselves. They were progressing so fast and becoming quickly independent, but they still loved for me to baby them. Reign made it inside first, but only because Riaan's attention was caught by how the door opened and closed. It was almost like he studied it as if he knew how it was happening. I picked him up and carried him the rest of the way inside because Damon's crazy ass was about to pull off.

"Can I get the babies in their seats first?" I called out.

"You are a top-flight babysitter, so I think you can do it while moving," Damon said before shutting the small door leading upfront.

"I should have let Reign keep on slapping you," I laughed. Blossom already had food on the table and moved to help me get the twins in their seats. I looked at what she had put together and almost died. Blossom had a plate of shredded chicken big enough for an adult in front of each chair. She also had a bowl of skittles for them and cups full of sweet tea.

"What in the–" I cut myself off and just knew Damon had something to do with this mess.

"Damon said this is what they needed to grow stronger, faster," Blossom smiled. The twins already had their chubby hands on the chicken and shoved it into their mouths. I didn't even try to take that away, but I quickly grabbed the skittles before they realized it was candy. I grabbed the two sippy cups and diluted them both with bottled water.

"Blossom, Damon is an idiot. That is way too much sugar for them and if they weren't tearing that chicken up, I might have cut the serving back a little.

"He said the colorful things were fruit. Fruit is good for children."

"How about I give you the rundown on what is good for kids after you tell me what the hell is going on," I said. I sat the cups back down, and they both reached for them simultaneously. I looked at Toya, sitting facing the window, but I could tell she wasn't really present. I looked at Quinn, who was watching her like a predator watching its prey.

"That is a fair trade, and you should know anyway," Blossom said. I was counting down in my mind when Quinn would move, and it wasn't long after I hit ten that he moved.

"LaToya! Get up. I think you have something you need to get off your chest."

"I don't know who the hell you think you are talking to, Quinn, but I will fuck you up. True Alpha or naw, I will light you on fire," she snapped. I could tell the flex in her jaw that she knew snapping when Quinn got like this was the wrong move. So when he reached down and yanked her short butt out of the seat, it was not a surprise. The door slammed, and I looked back at Blossom.

"Shani, what do you know about Necromancers?"

Chapter 14
Quinn

I dropped LaToya to her feet and slammed the door shut. "Silence the room."

"I don't know who you are thinking you are talking to, Quinn Savir, but it ain't me! I don't have time for this shit right now. These bastards are out here attacking children, raising the dead, and kidnapping people! What if that boy and his family had been Garrett? What if it were him, Quinn?" She cried.

"I know a lot of shit has happened, but you been talking real slick, so I'm going to need you to chill the fuck out," I gritted.

"I know you fucking lying right now. I am not one of your wolves! They are fucking with my family, Quinn, and I will not lose anyone else!"

"I get it, LaToya. I do, but I will need you to put up the spell," I calmly said. I was just as pissed the fuck off as she was, but I knew we had to get our minds together. "Your anger and being rash about shit is what they all want. They want us fucked up in the head and fighting."

"Fuck that shit! I am so done with trying to do things the

right way. The bitches who follow along with this dumb shit will get it too!"

"LaToya! Do it now," I growled. I moved closer to her and grabbed her chin, forcing her to look at me. I needed her to see I was just as angry as she was and that we had to be smart about our shit. After what Blossom said, things began to click into place for me. Yes, they wanted Garrett, but they did get his father, so I didn't think he was meant to be killed that night.

"It's done. Now, let me go," LaToya snarled as her skin heated beneath my touch.

"Baby—"

"No, I'm going to kill them," LaToya gritted as every emotion she felt poured through our bond. It was almost an overload because of what I was feeling, but whatever she put out, I knew I could take that shit.

"No, not without thinking first. Not without knowing full well what you are doing and figuring out who was part of it and who was forced into participating in the bullshit," I snapped. I grabbed LaToya's wrists and slammed her right into the door. I know it didn't hurt her by any means, but it shocked her enough to cut through the anger. I caged her with both hands on either side of her petite body. "You are not going anywhere in this condition right now. You and I will work through this shit so we both can think clearly. You're going to throw your anger all at me, and I'll fucking take it because that is what I do. Then, I'm going to fuck you so long and hard that you won't remember your own fucking name because you'll be too busy screaming mine. That way, when you finally calm the fuck down, we'll deal with the Witches, Warlock, and whoever else needs our attention. We will figure this shit out, and we find the real Tucker and his son."

I can see my words affecting my wife by how her eyes glowed sea-green and her nose flared. "No. Fuck that!"

That seemed to set off the wolf inside of me. I felt it

banging against me like my thumping heart trying to figure out how and why my Mate rejected me. She knew the Alpha in me hated more than anything else when she wasn't listening or thinking things through. It seemed like she didn't care, but her little ass would, soon enough.

"Don't tell me that you don't want this or that you don't want me right now. I can scent the need in you, LaToya, even if you don't want to admit it. It's all good, though."

LaToya's breath hitched as I ran my nose from her shoulder up to her neckline before settling on her jaw. All the while, I'm inhaling her sweet scent that drove me insane. I could feel her body shaking as I lightly touched her skin with my tongue. I could practically hear her heart beating wildly as I groaned. "Jesus, LaToya, I can fucking smell your arousal, so don't you tell me no, because I know when you're lying."

"So what! It doesn't matter, Quinn. I'm not changing my mind about this mess. When we get there, and I go deal with the council, I am burning the entire realm to the fucking ground," she whispered.

"No."

"My family sent Warlocks, Witches, and demons after our children. Who knows how many other families they have done that to that didn't survive or have people in their corner as we do? They went after Garrett before we knew him, Quinn, and if they got him, he wouldn't be with us! I hate that I am happy that he wasn't taken. What the fuck kind of person does that make me," she choked out. "Then tonight happened. All those pups and cubs there. Our children yet again were there, and they...they could have gotten hurt."

"Yes, but we were there to make sure it didn't happen because that is what this family does. We will find them and make them pay for what they did and have done," I promised. It was the truth, and once we had all responsible, she could burn them all to the ground while I would help her do it. I contained my wolf, and I could feel it prowling, ready to pounce and rip those bitches in half for what they have done to my wolves and for causing my Mate to feel this way. "That being said, I can't let you go out like this when you aren't thinking clearly, babe. When emotion and magic get involved, nothing good ever happens. I will not put you at risk, so if it means taking your anger out on me, then give it to me. We all have anger about this shit, baby. Even me, but not all of you, can burn cities to the ground or open a portal to Hell and leave them to their fates. Innocent people would be involved, then what?"

"I can't...I can't think straight, Quinn," she shook her head, trying to escape. I caught her wrists when she tried pushing me away, but I pinned her wrists tightly above her head. It caused her to gasp, especially when I pressed my huge body right into hers. Each time she took a deep breath, her breasts were pressed against me.

She rocked her hips, squeezing her thighs together to get enough pressure to ease that ache between her legs.

"I know," I gritted. LaToya's every movement had me pressing harder against her so she could feel how hard I was for her. "So take that temper and lay it on me. If you have to unleash whatever is going on in that pretty little head of yours, then give it to me. Give it to your Mate. Give me all you fucking got, and I promise that I will give it to you right back. I can take it," I growled. I knew LaToya needed an outlet for this anger, or all that power she held would go nuclear, especially since Nuriel wasn't here to help contain it. She moaned my name and tilted her hips, trying to hit that spot she needed. I thickened even further. "I want to take it from you, LaToya. So give it to me."

LaToya opened her mouth, probably arguing or beating herself up for something out of her control, but I would not let it get that far. I crushed my lips against hers, making her moan as she sucked on my tongue. Instantly, her shoulders sagged and it was easy to let go because my Mate needed this from me. She knew I could take it and handle her mouth and attitude, so once she got it through her head, this was how it would be. She quickly got lost in our kiss. I needed to fuck the anger out of her now, and at this rate, it may take us getting through a few states before she could pull it together. Hell, it may take me that long not to let her go off, and we all wipe out everyone we came across.

LaToya whimpered and then let out a long moan. I let my tongue dive straight inside her mouth because I needed her to forget. At least for a moment. Truthfully, my wolf is on the brink of losing it as well, but I need to stay calm for my Mate. She opened her legs for me to settle between as I used my knee to slowly grind against her clit.

The dress she had on was just in the way now. I maneuvered her wrist into one hand and used the other to unbutton her dress, revealing a sheer red bra. I squeezed her breast, drawing out another moan. The rough pad of my thumb slowly traced circles over her nipple, poking proudly at me. They were already ready for my undivided attention.

I growled while slowly kissing trails away from her mouth and down to the fabric of her dress. I latched onto her nipple through the thin fabric, causing her to cry out loudly. She twisted in my grip, and I let her go. LaToya's fingers find their way to the back of my neck and press me tighter into her body.

My hand trailed down, finding her soaked as I stroked her clit through her panties. LaToya whimpered as she arched her back to feed me her breasts while clawing at the hem of my shirt to expose my back before using her nails and digging right into my skin. I could feel the heat in her blood building, and it would have burned me, if I didn't carry the Twice Marked bond.

"Fuck, Quinn," she groaned. Her anger and hurt still saturated the space. I knew she had to deal with it and get it all out before dealing with anyone else.

"That's right," I snarled. "Give me all that anger, and I'll fuck it out of you."

With that said, I continued teasing her while she still was dressed. I knew that would frustrate her enough that her brain would start to think of ways how she could make me tear them off her body. I know she was ready to lose it from the way she thrashed her head and moaned. That is precisely what I wanted from her at this point. I wanted her on the brick of insanity before I gave her what she needed, before I gave us what we both needed at this moment. My saliva had stained through her dress, but I don't think she even cared at this point as she stared at me with lust-filled eyes. I knew I had her where. If she didn't give a shit about her clothes, then I had her right where I wanted her mind. I wanted her only to think of us and nothing else.

"You like that, LaToya?" I questioned rhetorically as I slowly drew lazy circles onto her swollen clit through her panties. I can smell her arousal practically filling up the room, making me throb, while thinking about sliding into her core. I was already leaking pre-cum, so I knew I couldn't wait too much longer. I had to claim her and mark her again.

"Yes, please...Quinn," she cried. "Fuck me already."

I damn sure was about to give her what she wanted. I pulled away, slinging my shirt across the room in one fluid motion. From the look in her eyes, I knew that my eyes were now midnight black and the ring was glowing red. I stood panting as I stalked over to her like a wolf, ready to feast on every inch of her body.

We wanted no more foreplay, especially, not with our intensity right now. I grabbed LaToya in a fast motion and tossed her on the bed.

"Turn around and place your hands on the headboard with

your ass up." It mainly was a growl, but she understood exactly what I said and wanted because her short ass wasted no time.

I waited as she did what I instructed before I dropped over her and kissed the back of her neck. My Mate had too many clothes, and I wanted nothing between us. I balled up the back of her dress and pulled it once, sharply ripping the dress off. I knew later she would be on her shit, but right now, all I could see, taste, and smell were the juices running down her legs.

"Quinn, please, I need you," she whimpered. I slid her drenched panties down her ebony legs until they stopped at her ankles. I groaned at the sight of her wetness before hooking my fingers and pulling them entirely off, leaving her in nothing but a pair of heels. I lightly trailed my fingers up her ass and smiled at how she jolted for me before settling behind her, gripping cheeks and squeezing.

I removed one hand and moved it to my belt buckle, unclasping it before sliding my jeans and boxers off. I was hard as fuck and throbbing, pre-cum gathering at the tip as I edged us both between sane and insanity. I let my hands caress her legs while reaching around to insert one finger inside her wet opening.

"Oh fuck! Quinn, just, please—" she said, bucking and trying to grind against my finger to give her the release she wanted. I pulled out, and she moaned at the loss of it. I could feel the heat of her blood and core as she burned hotter. I licked my lips as I spread her cheeks to see her glistening slit that was ready for me.

"I got you," I chuckled.

I let go and wrapped my hands around her waist, tilting her ass up the way I wanted it. My clawed hands traced her skin as new markings appeared on her body.

"Fuck me!"

I smirked, then growled as I slammed into her, sucking

back the hiss as I cursed at the tight grip she had on me. I moaned as her core wrapped around me like a vise. "Quinn!"

"Fuck, baby! Take what you want," I groaned. LaToya moaned as she began throwing it back, letting her set the pace. She took what she wanted. I leaned back, watching her move, but I knew I wouldn't be able to let that shit last for long. I needed to take control. I had to for us both. She wouldn't be able to cum like she wanted if I didn't. She knew it, and so did I, from the beginning of *us*. I tightened my grip on her hip and took control, quickly picking up the pace. I pounded into her faster, each thrust making her breasts bounce for me. The slapping of skin to skin filled the room, and I couldn't hear anything else but that and her screaming my name repeatedly.

"Oh, God! Don't stop, Quinn," she moaned. I leaned over her, trailing the flat of my tongue up her spine to the crook of her neck, lightly biting down onto her delicate skin. I felt the heat before I realized her entire body was on fire. Her magic covered us both, and I moved deeper inside her core, only slowing down to make sure she felt every inch. LaToya's flames did nothing to me as I let my hand reach around to flick a nipple. "Quinn," she moaned as I continued to mark her in the spot where I first claimed her as my Mate. I knew it brought her many new sensations because I felt it throughout the bond. I pulled back and growled while wrapping her hair in my fist. Pulling her head back, I made her back arch beautifully for me as she ultimately became lost in us. The markings glowed a burning red, the same shade as the ring in my eyes. "Please."

"I love you, LaToya," I groaned out at the way she tightened around me. She shuddered at my words, taking her higher with each thrust as she nodded furiously.

"I love you," she moaned. She craned her head back so her eyes could stare into mine, pushing me to the edge when I saw her finally letting go. I could see clarity in her eyes and feel the difference in her energy. I felt it throughout our bond and I could feel the anger dissipating.

"I want you to cum for me."

"Yes!"

I needed to see her face and feel her legs wrapped around me. I pulled out with that in mind, making her cry out at the loss of contact once more. I turned her around and tossed her back onto the bed. Her flame never dulled or burned anything around us. I didn't even wait for her to catch her breath before ramming my length back into her. Then, reaching down, I flick my fingertips over her swollen clit, making her dig her stiletto heels into my thigh in the process.

I slightly withdrew from her body, teasing her, before driving straight back into her core. Her tight sheath wrapped around my length and compressed. LaToya felt as if she got tighter, attempting to hold me in place as I dived into her again and again. I moved my hand from her clit and grabbed her leg, prompting her to wrap them around me. Her heels dug into my back with each thrust. "Quinn, Quinn, oh my—," she screamed. LaToya cried my name while clawing at my back as if she could fit my entire body inside herself. The flames grew hotter and brighter as she moaned while I ground into her core.

Fuck, I loved that fire inside of her and when it comes out in pleasure. Her entire body started quivering as I hit that little spot that I knew she loved. I had worked her into a frenzy as I repeatedly teased that spot. Her eyes could barely open as I worked the building orgasm out of my Mate.

"Quinn," she cried as she licked her swollen lips. "I'm, I'm, oh fuck, I'm—"

"I know," I snarled before stroking her sensitive clit, making her fall entirely off the cliff I placed her on, and it's the last straw to send her over the edge. A long, drawn-out-piercing scream rang loud, and I had no clue if she managed to hold on to the silencing spell, but I didn't give a fuck. My nose flared as I kept pumping harder, fucking her through her orgasm in a chase for my own relief.

Hell, I didn't know if I could stop as I relentlessly pounded into her, as the wet slapping sound filled the room. Sometimes, stamina is everything, but right now, I want to completely lose myself to my wife, the love of my life.

My *Mate.*

My balls drew up when her inner muscles clamped down even harder as she dug her heels just enough into my skin to break it. I came inside her with a loud feral noise that even scared me, giving her all I was worth. I coated her insides with my thick cum as I kept rocking into her, crushing her as I lay kisses all over my Mate before capturing her lips.

Neither one of us said anything for a while as we caught our breath. I scooped LaToya's body up in my arms, and her heels fell from her feet. I carried her into the medium-sized bathroom to clean her up. She was barely awake, which is exactly how I wanted her to be so she could rest. Once she was rested and her mind clear, then we could plan. Only then will we take revenge on those who dared to fuck with our family and people.

CHAPTER 15
LATOYA

"*You know nothing, child. You are a child that should have never existed. You, who I should have killed in your mother's womb. You who will die just like the bitch whose soul I now possess. Your time is coming, LaToya Aja Grey!*"

My eyes opened wide as I snapped awake from the pressure in my mind. I blinked a few times, trying to clear my thoughts from the disturbing whispers in my dream. Once my eyes focused, I saw a small sticker on the panel of a black rooster with a company name. I shook my head as the words became apparent the more I awakened. The whispers spoke more words than usual, but that wasn't quite right cause I knew for a damn fact that this wasn't like the whispers I usually hear. I took in a deep breath as I sat up and swung my legs to the side of the bed. I ached in all the right places, and I wished I could live in that moment, but the cruel words replayed in my thoughts now that I was fully awake. Who the fuck was that, and how in the hell did they have my mother's soul? I knew it was not Ellen or a voice I had heard before. I looked around, saw my dress lying torn in the trash, and sucked my teeth. I wanted to call my grandmother and ask her who else had a fixation on our family, but something told me that this had nothing to do with being a Grey Witch. I also didn't want to reach out right now because I did not want anyone or thing to trace that contact. After my mother died, I needed my grandparents safe from the dangers of the world I now live in.

I stood up and moved to my luggage to grab something to wear. The words were fucking with me, and if something held my mother's soul, I would find them and kill their ass as well. I shoved my legs in a pair of black mid-rise skinny jeans and grabbed a black long-sleeved jersey t-shirt with gold writing that read *"Warning! Hot Witch Walking"* on the front. I ran down everything I could remember of the night my mother was killed, but I couldn't figure out who this voice belonged to. I screamed in my head because this is when talking to Rhonda or Aja came in handy. I had neither one of them anymore to get their opinions. I opened my other suitcase and pulled out my Fendi black leather wedge booties with the gold heel. I stood up after pulling them on and exited the room. As soon as I opened the door, Quinn, Blossom, and Shani were standing on the other side like they were trying to get inside.

"LaToya! What the fuck happened?" Quinn questioned. He held the twins, who had tears in their eyes as they looked at me. I did not know what the hell was happening, but I was getting a bad feeling.

"I...I don't know. Wha—"

"Toya, we couldn't get inside the room. The twins were screaming and crying for you, and we all tried to get inside, but we could not. It was almost like a wall, with nothing on the other side. I couldn't even open a gate to get inside," Blossom stated. I looked at her, then back to Quinn as he spoke softly to the twins.

"Something was in my head. In my dream. I don't know what happened or who the fuck it is messing with me. Let me hold my babies," I said, pushing through them to get to Quinn.

"I couldn't get inside LaToya. Nothing should be able to keep me away from you," he grunted. Riaan and Reign both practically jumped out of Quinn's arms and into mine, and I held them close.

"I know, babe. We will make sure it will never happen again when we handle this. I will figure it out," I promised. I could see the fear in his eyes and feel the wolf inside of him clawing to get out and scent me. I moved closer as I kissed my babies when a phone began to play a song. I knew it wasn't mine, and it couldn't be Blossom's because I set her phone on vibrate. She hated the sounds and the tones they made. Shani seemed to snap out of it, and she looked me over once more before pulling out her cell.

"Hello."

"Shani! It's Journee. I have been calling Toya and Quinn and not getting an answer. Where is Toya?" I frowned at her tone because she sounded as if she were panicking.

"I don't know, but she can hear you. What's wrong?"

"Zaccai! Zaccai is gone! The Warlock took him! He kidnapped my child!"

"What!"

"They took him! After everything went down and we finished the wards, I looked for him. Leodora said he followed her to the room, but there were so many others she just thought he was with the other pups. I did a location spell on him, but it keeps jumping! I can't get a lock on his location, and when I do, I cannot make a portal to get to him. Something is blocking me from my child! Toya, Premier, please! Please help me!"

"Stay on the line and listen to everything I say. I will find Zaccai and bring him home, Journee. You have my word. Are any of the other children missing?"

"No, no, everyone is accounted for, but I can't sit here and do nothing while that...that bastard has my child!"

"Yes, you can, and yes, you will, because that is what is needed to save him. Make a circle, sit in the middle of it, and remove your necklace. Hold it in your palm and do what I say. I will bring him back to you."

I looked at Quinn and saw the beast staring back at me. His entire body vibrated with anger, and I knew I might have to calm him down this time before he went off that ledge I stood on recently. I turned to Shani, and she was already there, taking the twins from my arms. That was like a punch to the gut, but I knew what needed to be done. I closed my eyes and used the bond I held with each Circle member. I found the flickering maroon light of Zaccai's power. I also felt the raw evil energy that surrounded the boy. I pulled on that thread until I felt the edge of Zaccai's mind. I felt the whispers creeping back, but I let them inside this time. I did exactly what that demon told me to do and owned it. This gift was a part of me, so I could use it as I saw fit. There was no need to be afraid of something I could control. I ripped through the souls that clung to Georgy and pulled the location from them. I didn't want Zaccai to be startled by me looking through his eyes, so I used that bitch Gregory instead. I stared into light brown eyes and a face much like my grandmother, but only younger. Zaccai was with Ellen and they stood in the house where I was born.

"That bitch!" I screamed, and then I felt pain as Georgy felt my presence. Then Ellen focused and smiled.

"It's about time we end this, niece. I am tired of waiting and playing these games. Bring your ass home, LaToya Grey. I am about ready for the power that should belong to me," Ellen sneered. She held up a hand, then brought it down sharply. That movement slammed into my consciousness, pushing it from Gregory, and slammed back into my body. It didn't hurt physically, but it felt like someone had stabbed me in the eye mentally. I sucked in a breath, but I felt warm arms wrap around me as Quinn pushed healing energy inside my body. It eased the pain, but not the anger I was feeling.

"I'm good, Quinn. Damon, stop the truck!" I screamed.

"What are you thinking?"

"We are going to the Other Realm. Ellen may think I am a young inexperienced Witch, but that will be the mistake that gets her head blown clean off her shoulders," I snarled. Damon hit the brakes, and this big ass RV slammed to a stop. I heard horns and screeching of vehicles, but I blocked it all out. The door swung open, and I looked into Damon's golden eyes.

"It takes time to form a portal to that realm. You said Rhonda had to prepare for it and have someone on the other side to let you cross," Quinn said.

"Yes, that is true, but not for a Hell Gate. I know the route, which is all Blossom needs, right?" I questioned. We both looked at Blossom and saw her using her fingers to draw circular patterns as if she was making a painting.

"This will take an enormous amount of power to do, LaToya. We would all need to move at once, so the best way to do it is to drive us right through the portal, then the gate," Blossom asserted. "You will drain your power in doing this, Toya. Doing this spell will pull on your magic because we are stepping into a locked realm from the other side. Are you sure they will be there?"

"Yes." I knew I was right. Ellen may believe she did some trickery in pushing me out, but those souls saw and heard everything. No matter if they were bound to Gregory or not, they didn't belong there, and I was the one to send their ass on to the other side where they belonged.

"Let's get it done then," Quinn growled. "I will give you the power stored inside of me." I nodded, but I knew that might not be able to happen. We would be on a different plane, which changes things even for a Twice Marked bond. Quinn furrowed his brows as he stared at me, but I looked away, not wanting to waste any more time. We had to get Zaccai out of there, and soon.

"Shani lock the twins down in their seats. Do not leave their side for anything. I need you and Blossom to protect them at all costs. We may be just moving through Hell, but they will know it, and them bitch ass demons will try some bullshit," I said. I turned around and spotted a clear area close to the front. I saw Damon smiling tightly with two sets of fangs, and his eyes bled to full black.

"I got it, Toya," Shani stated while I sat crossed-legged on the floor. I took in a breath, staring straight ahead.

"All I got to say two-short is I never thought I would be the one actually to drive the bus to Hell. At least we are not wearing gasoline draws," Damon chuckled. He turned to face the front, and as I slipped into calmness, I saw his smile fade and his jaw tense. I felt Quinn as he settled behind me, wrapping his arms and legs around me. His nose was in the crook of my neck, and he breathed deeply. I closed my eyes, ready to end this and bring these Witches, Warlocks, and whatever else that thought it could fuck with us. Thinking about Hell had me thinking about my father, Baron, and who he warned me about. If the voice was his wife and she had plans to fuck with me, I would bury her like I did Valerie. *Brijit* seems to be just the Goddess of Death now, and she wanted to kill me. She could bring it too because she didn't know LaToya Aja Grey Savir.

"Journee repeat after me. *Time crumbles into dust, invisible forces, and ethereal silence. We pass through space and step into the mouth of the skies. We pass through the womb of water as we walk into the truth of what we are and are meant to become. Time crumbles into dust, invisible forces, and ethereal silence. We pass through space and step into the mouth of the skies. We pass through the womb of water as we walk into the truth of what we are and are meant to become.*"

Deadly Secrets

I FELT the sudden drain and knew it was time for us to move. I opened my eyes and raised my hands out in front of me. "Damon! Drive!" I gritted as the largest portal I ever made ripped open in front of us. Damon hit the gas, and I could hear Blossom speaking in a language that just sounded wrong. I couldn't understand it and it made me feel as if I shouldn't even attempt it. Her words were almost like a growl mixed with clicking noises. I shook my head as a bead of sweat trailed down my temple, but I felt Quinn tighten his hold on me.

"I changed my mind! I do not want to go back back to Hell!" Damon roared. I felt the speed pick up, though, as we slammed through the portal. Everything flashed a bright blue and green as the portal swallowed the entire RV, but it suddenly shifted. Outside turned an ashy gray as the world changed to something resembling a post-apocalyptic world that smelled of despair. Millions of eyes of demons turned toward us and I felt more fear than the last time I was there.

"Keep going!" Blossom's voice sounded distant, but it echoed through the space of the RV. We were driving directly toward the mass of demons, and my eyes widened as one stood up taller than the rest of them. There was no face, only black pits for eyes. Its massive head tilted as I felt something press hard against my mind and shields.

"Cambions."

The voice in my thoughts raked against my brain as it pressed hard. I heard Riaan let out a wail, and I instantly reacted. I felt Quinn shove energy into me simultaneously and I pushed that bitch back. The mental slap flung the giant demon aside, making the rest roar as they charged the RV. Before they were about to crash into us, everything went black as a peaceful feeling filled the space. I exhaled as we popped out into a world where the sky was green with streaks of different colors and the four suns shined in front of us. Damon slammed on the brakes as the RV slid on the lush green grass, but he expertly controlled the spin-out. We stopped just at the edge of a large cliff that overlooked water in the shade of a shimmering pearl.

"Oh my God!" Shani panted. I looked back and saw her protectively hovering over the babies as her eyes darted side to side. I frowned as she looked as if she was fading in and out, but when I blinked a few times, it didn't happen again. "How did Taria survive in that place?" She asked no one or everyone. Quinn's grip loosened from my waist, and he stood up, pulling me with him. He made sure I was steady before moving to the twins to check them over. I wobbled slightly and saw Blossom do the same.

"I don't know. I guess because it's Taria," I said weakly. I could feel the drain of my magic, but I prayed that this land's saturated magic that filled this dominion would solve the issue.

"That girl would have died if I hadn't rescued her," Damon grunted. I saw him wiping blood from an already healing cut on his forehead.

"Technically, I rescued the both of you from the cell, and then she saved you on multiple accounts," Blossom said. I felt weak as fuck, but there was no time for all that shit. I blinked fast, trying to clear my head, and moved over to the twins to kiss them. I regretted taking them from the school, but it had to be done. They would not be safe all the time, and I knew as long as they were with me and their father, we would keep them safe.

"Bullshit! If it weren't for me, Shade, your ass would have been burned by that blinding ass light, and Taria would have bought her ticket too many times to count," Damon chuckled. I could hear him standing and moving around. I looked at Quinn and could feel that he felt the same as I did as we both kissed our children.

"Toya, you will need to arm up as much as possible. Marcus sent these with us for you to use," Blossom said. I didn't turn around as I used the last bit of Magic. I could feel it place a protective barrier over the RV. I knew it wasn't as strong as it should be, but it would buy Shani and Blossom time to put up a defense.

"What in the hell did that torture send?" I sighed. I turned to face Blossom as she held out black fingerless gloves. I reached out, taking them from her, and looked them over. I felt Damon come up beside me and lean over my shoulder. "Get your hot ass breath off me." He proceeded to put his chin on my head. If I had the energy to spare, I would have set his ass on fire!

"Heat rises, so you ain't talking about me ankle bitter," he said. He reached out and snatched the gloves out of my hand and inspected them. "Fucking Marcus. How the fuck did he get his hands on something like this?"

"Boy! Give them to me!" I shouted and snatched them back. There was a circle stitched on each palm, with symbols of each element. The top of the gloves had words that seemed slightly out of focus. They began to make sense to me when I noticed that they were written the same pattern as the markings on my arms. "Wha—what is this?" I whispered. After laying the twins down on the bed, Quinn came out of the room. I prayed that they would just sleep through all of this and wake up once we returned home. Quinn made his way over to me and took a look at the gloves.

"When I was studying up on this magic shit, I asked Marcus for some books. He provided me with a lot of material, and I found instructions on how to make a way to harness your energy. It was more of a theory but—"

"Oh, that shit is not a theory at all. These gloves belonged to the first of your kind. I know this because I found them a long fucking time ago. I gave them to Caleb for research to find the rightful owner. Marcus must have noticed what I see now," Damon nodded. I rarely heard him this serious, making me look up at him.

"What do you see?"

"You see and feel it as well, Toya. You can see the pattern that only you carry."

I opened my mouth, but it snapped shut as the whispers crashed into my mind with such force I thought my head would explode. There were many before, but now there were millions.

"LaToya!" Quinn shouted as he caught me.

"I'm good! They know we are here." I looked around and knew it was time. I couldn't do any of this alone, and Taria knew that. She sent the best people who could help, and I trusted that. I had to trust in myself and our abilities to see this shit through. "Shani and Blossom, protect the children at all costs," I ordered. I looked at Quinn and saw the confirmation of what we needed to do. I hated being apart from him, but it was what had to be done.

"Damon and I will deal with the Warlock. You need to take care of Ellen," Quinn growled.

"What about the other Witches and Warlocks that are following them?" Shani snarled. Damon stood up straight and cracked his neck while looking at Quinn.

"You better kill that soul-stealing bastard Quinn. I will deal with the Witch bitches and Whorelocks. I need to kill some shit anyway. Things have been too quiet lately," Damon chuckled darkly.

I nodded and then realized this fool finally said the quiet part out loud, but I agreed with him this time.

"The fact that I agree with you, Damon, is scary as hell," I laughed. The whispering became more of a shrill scream, but a buzzing and chittering sound started.

"Fucking Cicadas!" Damon said, looking out of the window. "Oh shit. This is about to get interesting," he said as lengthy groans that sounded like every zombie movie I ever watched came from all directions. "This bitch brought the undead with his ass!"

My eyes widened, but Damon was already gone leaving the door swinging wide open. I looked at Quinn as I pulled on each glove and nodded. Then we followed Damon *"Demon"* Vaughn out the door.

CHAPTER 16
DAMON

It felt so good to let the inner demon out to play. Soon as I left the RV, I covered my hands in energy and sliced clean through the neck of an ***Akhkhazu.*** There were so many of them that I knew I would be able to vent this frustration of not dealing with the fucking Necrolock myself. I also knew that the dog could deal with it while I watched his Mates's back. This wasn't only personal to me but also him as the Alpha. I shoved my other hand through the chest of an ***Akhkhazu*** and yanked out the heart before throwing energy at the approaching undead wave that was coming toward the RV. I felt that we were back in that pit in Hell, but it was more colorful. That only proved that just because it was pretty didn't mean it wasn't full of shit.

"You could have waited," Toya said from beside me. She threw a fireball into the undead, but it didn't do as much damage as it would typically have.

"I had to clear the way. You need to figure out what the hell you should do to fix that if you go up against your Auntie," I laughed while taking a bug by the head and throwing it. Its body hit others that were pulling themselves up from the ground. The body's sound as it hit them was like the pins in a bowling alley. "Strike!"

"Yeah, well, I have no clue how to do that, but that bitch is dead, dead either way! If I have to beat her ass with my fist, that will happen," Toya shouted. I turned and grabbed Toya by her shirt as I shot an energy blast toward the approaching undead on her left. What I wasn't expecting were the loud gunshots that rang out. I looked back, and Toya was blowing huge holes in the chest of the ***Akhkhazus*** that were getting closer.

"Who the hell would teach you how to use a gun? They know you are crazy, right?"

"Me! You are the psycho here, Damon, not me. Let's not get it twisted."

"It had to be Marcus. Had to be," I muttered. The Desert Eagle was way too giant for her infant hands, but she accurately shot it, making me have to let it go and let her have her moment. With each shot, I noticed with each ***Akhkhazus*** she hit, a wave of magical energy would blow the others away if they were near the target. "We need to move away from the RV!"

Toya shot a few more before I wrapped my arms around her waist and ran toward the dead bodies walking. I knew from the moment I spotted them that they weren't like the ***Akhkhazus***. They have tortured souls made for walking again and cannot move on as they should.

"Wait! Wait where–" Toya screamed. I didn't say a word because I knew what I had to do, and putting her in the middle of the chaos may help her jump-start the power hidden deep inside her body, mind, and soul. She was more than just a Witch that could command all the elements but one who walks between life and death.

"Remember those lessons I was teaching you?"

"Yes, but you didn't teach me a damn thing!"

I landed in the middle of the slack lifeless faces. Before they could react to our presence, I dropped the little person to her feet.

"Get down!" I roared and slammed both fists into the ground. Sparks of green energy connected to the undead surrounding us and they all let out a hoarse scream.

"Oh my God! What kind of scream is that?" Toya shouted. I pushed more energy into the ground, letting the magic-soaked world use my energy to attack what shouldn't be in this realm.

"Listen to me, LaToya! Remember what I said to you and think about who you are! You are not just a Witch that commands fire or the daughter of the Grey bloodline. You are more than that. You can't be afraid of death or fear the grave when it is you who can control it. Now go!" I growled. I felt my fangs hitting my chin as I roared. I raised both hands, letting them transform into claws. I swiped out, knocking over a dozen undead, giving Toya a path straight to the only building in this pocket dimension.

"Damon, I–I don't know if–" she stammered, but there was no time.

"Yes, you can. I know you can. Zaccai is there, and you will overcome anything for family," I gritted. It felt as if she stared at me for minutes when it was only seconds before she sprinted for the stone building.

"Don't ever tell anyone we had this touching moment, Demon."

Her voice in my mind sounded serious, but I could hear the amusement and fear. I wasn't about all that touchy-feely shit, but I knew when someone needed encouragement.

"If I can still do this after everything I have done, you can and will do what needs to be done. Look toward the sky."

I pulled back from her mind because I had to concentrate. I let the power go as I fell to my knees and the undead bodies dropped to the ground. I felt the ripping of skin and bones reforming as I clawed at the ground. I felt the ground shaking as more and more undead along with the fucking Cicadas, came for us. I let go of the pain as the mint green energy blasted out of my body. Wings burned their way through my shirt, spreading across the ground. I shot up into the sky, looked down over the land, and saw Toya looking at me with wide eyes. I turned away and saw a line of Witches and Warlocks standing together, holding hands in the distance. The twisted back markings that once meant something were now corrupted by the tattoos of Necromancy. I knew I had to keep them away from Toya until she killed their source of black magic. They were powerful, but only because they drew their power from Ellen's deep well of magic. I had no clue where she was gaining this power, but we would get the answers and deal with that bastard next. I raised a hand toward the four suns in the sky, almost as if they belonged in this world. I waved a hand, and thick black clouds began rolling in, covering the sky as thunder rumbled in the distance. I waited for a beat, then pulled lightning from the sky to bring it crashing down in the center of the massive crowd heading for the RV.

~

Deadly Secrets

I FOLDED my wings tightly to my back and arrowed myself toward the Witches that broke away from their Circle. I knew they would go after Toya, and I couldn't let that happen. If she could get to Ellen and get this shit done with, none of them would have the power to keep their hearts beating.

"Shade, hundreds will be knocking at the door."

"Let them come. I have destroyed legions of demons, so this will be easy."

I wanted to see the swirl of her eyes as she spoke and watch her fight, but I couldn't. The grace she had when she wielded those swords and how that ass moved had me rushing to chop these fools' heads off so I could watch her from above. I landed on the ground in front of two Witches who thought they could attack Toya from behind. The little fir Witch got on my last nerve, but I wasn't about to let anyone take away my rival.

"Naw, that is not where your fight will be," I growled.

"Angels do not belong in the fight of this world," A Witch sneered. I cocked my head at her like she was stupid. Her short, tightly curled hair, was streaked with blood as if she hadn't washed the blood off from the last sacrifice.

"When did I say that I gave a fuck?" I snarled. I struck out with my clawed hand and took off her head. The body of the nameless Witch fell to the ground, and I grinned. Finally, I could kill someone without feeling so fucking wrong about it! "This is about to be lit as fuck!" I laughed as the other six Witches roared at me while they attacked. I opened my wings, letting myself fly back as a ball of blue energy streaked with black came at me. I leaned back, letting it fly over my head, and kicked out at the closest Witch to me.

"If we bring him to the chamber, imagine the power we will gain?"

"They want the children," another Witch said. I figured that she wished that she kept that shit to herself. I moved and caught the bitch by the throat and sank my fangs into her neck. I tore away from her, let her blood squirt out, hit the others in the face, and threw her about ten feet away into a tree. I heard her head crack when it made contact, but I was already moving. Blood covered my mouth and chest as I faced the other Witches. I knew my eyes burned gold and that I had a deranged smile spread across my face. I only knew it because I began to scent the fear coming from them.

"I'm not usually so bloodthirsty, but when you talk about my niece and nephew, I get hungry," I growled. I let the second set of fangs descend as I attacked. I grabbed a Witch and rose in the air faster than the others could track. This Witch was about my height, and she had some skill. Her forehead connected with mine as she shot a burning orange ball of energy into my shoulder. It threw me off slightly, but I corrected myself by dropping her to the ground. I knew that was what she thought she wanted, but I was about to show her why that course of action was wrong. I turned as she shot off blast after blast and I felt more coming from the others I left on the ground. I stayed in the air for one more second, then I dropped. I crashed into the undead, knocking away a good portion. I lifted one and used its body as a bat. The energy blast above me hit each other, creating a large boom as if a bomb went off. The magic meant for me returned to the senders, hitting them ten times harder. I flung the undead into three Cicadas crawling over the RV, then shot back up. More blasts came from the other magic users, but I wrapped my wings around my body while using telekinesis to keep myself floating in the sky. The energy slammed into my wings, then bounced back as a green light lit up the dark sky. The magic was tossed back at the others, but they managed to move before getting hit with their own attack. At least they were smart enough to move.

I looked down where the other Witches were and saw nothing but black scorch marks where they once stood. I opened my wings and reached up just as lightning struck. I grabbed onto it, turning the light purple bolt into a light green and gold mixture. I reared back and threw the bolt down on the pile of undead and blasted them into pieces. Blossom stood up from the pile holding a Witch that must have slipped past me. Her sword came down and cleanly cut the Witch across the throat. Then Blossom turned a half step, leaned back while still holding the Witch's head, and threw her off the cliff. I wanted to say something or join her in the mayhem we were creating, but I spotted A Warlock and Witch getting closer to the building. Toya entered. I was not about to let that shit go down. I pulled on energy and let it cover my entire body as I dove into the ground. The fall created a large crater between the two that were going after Toya and the building. I stood up and lifted back into the air. I caught the eyes of the Warlock. His dark brown hair and washed-out gray eyes burned with hate and irritation.

"You do not know who we are, do you? No idea who I am," the man grunted. "I am also a Grey and hold more power than you would ever imagine existing."

I raised a brow and started to laugh. The laughter built in my chest, coming out more demonic than I would want anyone else to hear, but no one that mattered was around to witness it.

"You, little boy, have no fucking clue who I am or what true power is, but let me show you," I chucked as I licked the tips of both sets of fangs. The blood of someone evil tasted so much sweeter when they realized the one they are up against is worse than they will ever be.

Chapter 17
Shani

The screams and noises coming from outside woke up the twins. They weren't crying but were more alert as they looked around. It was almost as if they could see what was happening outside the RV. All three of us looked up when we heard something crash above us. The buzzing and chittering sounds were almost overwhelming, but the groans had me freaked out. The smell of rotting meat, old blood, and despair seemed to cling to the air. It filled the RV like it was covered in the stuff. The RV rocked and I was slightly afraid it would get pushed off the cliff. Blossom had been gone for a minute, but her words still replayed in my mind.

"Quinn and Toya have placed all their trust in you to keep what matters to them the safest. This is a test of Will, Shani. Can you live up to what you were meant to be or let your old fears freeze you in place?"

"Sha-Sha," Riaan whispered. I turned to look at the twins, who stared up at me with love. I would do whatever it took to ensure they were protected, even if that meant giving my life for them.

"It's okay, baby. I will keep you safe," I said, touching their cheeks. I thought back to Blossom's words once more and knew that she was right, I had to try, but could I do it? I asked her that question, but she never had the chance to answer it. The RV shook once more, and I knew the protection spell Toya wrapped around it was failing. We knew this could happen, but I didn't know I would have to defend the babies alone. What if I fucked up, or one of them died because I was too slow? The instant anger and growl that came from me told me all I needed to know at that moment. I had to do this and get it right. I looked at Reign and Riaan as they stared back at me. They both looked at each other and began babbling as if they understood what each other was saying. "Okay, you two, stay right here, and I will be right back," I said as another loud crash came from the front. I prayed nothing was inside, but I cracked my neck in anticipation of a fight.

"Sha!" I looked back, and Reign stood up on the bed with eyes like her father staring back at me.

"Stay here, Reign. Stay together," I said. I moved for the door and closed it behind me as the RV rocked once again. The buzzing became louder as claws ripped the door away from the RV. I didn't wait until the damn bug made an appearance inside. I launched myself at it, knocking it back out of the door crashing into a dozen of them. Clawed, leathery hands gripped my arms and tried to pull them apart. Instead, I yanked them both together hard, making each creature slam into the other. I didn't stop to see if that managed to knock them out because more were coming. I heard a deep chuckling coming from the sky, making me look toward the sound. I swear I saw large maroon wings flying toward the only building I could see. I blinked as something touched my shoulder with cold fingers. I spun around and ducked low with my leg stretched, taking whatever it was down. I popped back up and twisted to the left, pulling out the blade Blossom gave to me. I sliced out, cutting the throat of a man who looked as if he shouldn't be able to walk, let alone attack someone. That is when I realized what was happening and heard the moans. I turned right as a hissing sound got louder, so I threw the blade, hitting the ***Akhkhazus*** in its beady red eye. I jumped straight up and used the heads of the undead and ***Akhkhazus*** to propel myself back toward the opening of the RV. I had gotten too far away, but before I leaped to get back inside, I grabbed the blade sticking out of its eye.

I dropped to the ground and let out a sidekick to knock out its knee, and shoved my fist through its chest. I pulled back and dropped the heart to the ground, and kicked the body over. I turned away and ran back for the opening and almost made it when something grabbed me by the ankle and began to pull me down. As the ***Akhkhazus*** tried to bring me beneath the dirt, everything moved faster. I scrambled for purchase on the ground when I saw not one but three of the undead enter the RV. "NO!" I roared as I used the blade to claw my way out of the hole it was trying to drag me into. I growled and felt my shift come over me, giving me more strength to get free. When I heard the pitch in the buzzing and chittering change, I knew something was up. I was partially shifted, using my enlarged clawed hand to dig in the dirt and pull.

I got my legs free and stood up fast to see a bigger Cicada-looking asshole standing atop the RV. I saw it as it dropped inside through the roof access portion, and I knew what would happen. "Hell No! Blossom? Quinn!" I cried as I leaped into the RV, clearing the two steps in one move. The undead seemed just as stupid as if they were zombies. They all stood facing the door where the twins were growling and groaning. I could feel the anger and fear for the twins fill me as everything went black. I could still see, but it was as if a golden haze filled my gaze. I could tell that the undead could not see me in the back of my mind because none of them reacted as I came up from behind. My arms and hands moved as if I weren't the one using them. I grabbed its head with ease and used my canines to sink into the next one's neck and ripped a hole in it. Thick black blood oozed out, but I wasn't done. I dug both claws into the undead back, pulled out the spine, and heard the scream. I saw the last undead with the bug, and they each had a twin. I roared and howled at the audacity that they believed they could touch my family.

"Sha, Sha!" Riaan cried. He waved his chubby fist in the air, and the undead moved. It slammed headfirst into the cabinets, making it release Reign. She fell to the floor crying, slid across the floor like an invisible force, and moved right into my arms. I picked her up, knowing it was Riaan who pushed his sister. Reign began to cry as she turned to look for her brother, only to see the Akhkhazus smashing through the side of the RV and leaping off the cliff. "Oh my God! Riaan!"

I TURNED in a circle to figure out what to do and wished someone was coming.

"Ri! Ri!" Reign cried as I stood there like a damn idiot. How could I let this happen? What would I tell Toya and my Alpha? I didn't know what to do!

"Quinn and Toya have placed all their trust in you to keep what matters to them the safest. This is a test of Will, Shani. Can you live up to what you were meant to be or let your old fears freeze you in place?"

Blossom's words rang in my mind, snapping me out of the spiral of thoughts I was traveling down. They trusted me to keep them safe and that is precisely what I will do. I heard buzzing and moans as the RV rocked again. I braced my feet apart and thought quickly. I couldn't leave Reign, and no one was coming because everyone was fighting. I was not the babysitter. I was family and the True Alpha's Pack member. The Delta. I refused to freeze when there was trouble, not this time. I would fight, or I would die fighting. I moved, almost slipping in the thick blood that covered the floor and pushing into the room. I grabbed the tactical front baby carrier out of the small closet. I laughed when Quinn brought this thing as if either one of the twins would stay in it long. I sat a wailing Reign on the bed and put the straps over my arms. I picked her up and stuck her inside, ensuring she was strapped in tightly.

"We are going to get your brother, Reign. Now I need you to be the big sister and not cry, okay?"

"Me, no cry! Want Ri!" Reign screamed. The tiny baby growl told me all I needed, and that was that this pup was good and pissed off. I ran and jumped out the same hole made by the Jeeper's Creeper's older brother. Now I wished that Cam, Toya, and Taria hadn't made me watch that movie because it was all I could see. I just prayed that it didn't eat body parts and use them as its own. We flew out the opening and right off the side of the cliff. The water was beautiful, but I knew they did not go in there.

I could scent Riaan through everything that was around me. The rot, blood, evil, and anger couldn't hide my baby boy from me. I reached out and dug my claws into the rock wall and slid down, making sure my stomach faced outward. Before losing momentum, I pushed off the wall and flipped to the beach below. I saw burned leathery flesh leaving a trail in the direction it took Riaan. It didn't try to take him underground, which told me someone was telling it what to do. I knew it wasn't the Warlock that Quinn dealt with, so it had to be another one or Witch. I pushed my body faster and realized I had slipped into the same state I had been in back at the Rayne property. I looked down, making sure it wasn't hurt. Reign and I saw her leaning her head back, staring at me.

"Ri, Ri."

"We will get him now, baby," I whispered. I looked up just as a blast of fire exploded ahead of us. I took a step, and we were out of the cliff's shadow when I realized how far we had traveled. I knew I would need to examine that later because we now faced the Witch that controlled the ***Akhkhazus.***

"You brought the other child right to me like a good little dog. Bring her over here to cousin Vernice," she smiled. The woman was brown skin with short blond hair. She was tall for a woman, at least six feet, and the black tattoos crawled over her body in a pattern not just for a Witch. It seemed like everyone here had already sold themselves for power. "Oh, I see you think I am one of them. No, no, see, that is where you are wrong, child. I am a true Necromancer, and I do not work for the Death whore they claim as a Goddess. I serve only one. *Idh,*" Vernice grinned. I knew what I was facing wasn't anything normal, and I knew that this bitch wasn't going to be easy to put down, but you best believe she would learn today not to fuck with my family, especially the twins.

"That bitch will die just like the rest who mess with us. Riaan! Light them up!" I roared. Riaan's entire body lit a bright red flame, setting everything around him on fire.

18 CHAPTER QUINN

I was used to the pain of transforming, and it came to me naturally, as if I were changing clothes. Breaking every bone in my body as it reformed itself in mere seconds wasn't something every shifter could do. At times, I couldn't get a hold of the uncontrollable urges I felt in my complete wolf form. I knew that some of my Alphas could take the third form just as I could, but none could take the form I used. The world was suddenly washed in red. My instincts kicked in, as I could not stop the wolf inside me. The fire that burned through my blood and soul was like an imprint of the magic LaToya left on me once we Mated. That took everything I was to a whole level. I was not worried about this Warlock or Necrolock because I was secure in my own power. There was no need to borrow, steal, or misuse the gifts given to me, so I knew his ass was about to get buried.

Despite my anger at what Gregory had done, I decided to speak to him in my human form. Once I did transform, there would be no more talking. I was not only trying to spare Gregory from being killed instantly but also out of caution. It would be harder to kill if the Necromancer ever got his hands on an Alpha wolf in complete wolf form. The power and knowledge that an Alpha wolf carries in their blood aren't for everyone.

The scent of rain was thick in the air, hinting of a storm brewing.

"Alpha Quinn," greeted a smooth voice.

I took a deep inhale, my nostrils filled with the stench of a corpse—the scent of death. The telltale smell of a Necromancer, but Gregory was nowhere to be seen.

"Cut the bullshit," I said.

"To what do I owe such a friendly visit?" Gregory's voice was quiet, soft. Like he was testing me, almost a whisper, to see how far my wolf abilities could be pushed.

"I'm not looking to chit-chat," I grunted, "there will be no trouble if you comply with me. Give me the soul and stop this shit you have going, and I will not kill you. Turn yourself over to your Premier now, and things may end differently."

I aimed to keep it simple, despite the intense rage burning in my chest. I wanted only one thing: to free Taj's departed soul, so his suffering would end, and he could no longer be used as some plaything or killing machine. I couldn't look Garrett in the face if I did not take care of his father right here and now. It would be hard enough to tell him what he knew was a lie, but the kid was resilient.

"And what exactly would I be complying with?" I heard the smile in Gregory's voice, showing mocking disinterest. He had no clue how lucky he was that it was me coming for him. It may not have been quick, but I wanted to free Taj as painless as possible.

"Taj." I started, holding back a growl that threatened to escape. "I want his soul."

The Necromancer chuckled, "ah." A gentle rustle of the leaves sounded from behind. I turned, meeting Gregory's green gaze that was tinged with a hint of swirling blackness. "And why would I do that? He has so much power in his blood. Something different about it gives me so much...life."

I knew what it was, but he did not precisely know what bloodline he held. That was one good thing because if he did, I was sure he would use that to bargain with any demon that showed interest.

I unsheathed my claws, and I was already on Gregory with impossible speed. I had lined a sharp claw over Gregory's unguarded throat, not cutting, but *very* close to it, "you are one stroke away from death," I answered, "if you are wise, you will trouble my Pack and my wife no further and hand me Taj's soul."

Gregory smirked, unfazed, eyeing the powerful claw, "What if I'm not wise?"

I clenched my jaw; because I did not have time for this. I pushed Gregory against a tree, "this isn't a game. You are fucking with my wolves, but what you will not do is fuck with my family."

Gregory's smile did not falter as the tree shook with the impact, "But, even if I wanted to give you his soul, it doesn't work that way. His body is bound to me now."

I ground my teeth together because I was afraid that he would say something like that. "Find. A. Way."

The Necromancer's stomach vibrated as he laughed darkly, "let me think..." This fool pretended to be deep in thought. Two, three seconds passed before he snapped from it with a smile, "no." It wasn't as if I expected anything less, but I still had to try if it saved Taj from any more pain. It wasn't only that, but I didn't want to draw on the Twice Marked bond because I knew LaToya was fighting her own battle.

I felt the rush of blood pumping into my head. I couldn't let this bastard fuck with me and make snap judgments. I lifted Gregory's collar, his legs dangled, and I raised a muscled arm to strike him. If he wouldn't help me the easy way, it was the hard way for his bitch ass.

"Unless..."

My ears twitched, listening, "continue."

"You give me something in return."

I didn't like where this was going, but I took the bait, lowering him, "like what?" I wanted to hear what he had to say and figure out his actual plan. Who were he and Ellen working for, and what did they want from my shifters?

A smile played on his lips, "*your* soul perhaps. Give up your body..." Gregory dropped his voice to a whisper. "To *me*."

I shot him a deadly glare, "are you insane? You know I won't do that. You are trippin if you believe I would ever let that shit down. Who truly wants my soul? Because my soul isn't anything you can handle."

Gregory scoffed. "My Goddess would work wonders with your soul and your Pack. Why does it matter to you because you have already failed Taj, didn't you? I wonder how long it will take for the Pack to realize you will fail them, too?"

The adrenaline rush pumped through me again. I felt my body heating up as the markings on my body turned from black to red. A crack sounded in my bones, showing my form was changing.

They want to use your soul to control your birthright. They will use it to control all wolf shifters and your Witch. She could not kill you and will never forgive anyone who does. Thus, it would tear apart the family you all have created to stand against what is coming.

I knew Kannuck's voice when he spoke, and he was right. How many factions were against us, and how many were working together to take us down? The only plan was to take us out any way possible, and it began long before we were born.

Gregory stared in awe, scanning me up and down as I tried

to fight back the wolf threatening to escape. I could feel the dark magic pulling at the call to my wolf as it tried to possess it, but that shit wasn't going down.

"Yes... change." Gregory leaned forward.

"No!" I snarled, a throaty growl resonating through him. My bones cracked, my skin ripped and reformed, and my build expanded. The pain was brief but intense, rippling away in seconds. I stopped myself from changing entirely, but I knew I had shape-shifted into my third form. My two legs were still stable enough to hold me up, and my arms were much like human arms but furred. I was bursting with overwhelming power and accompanied with long, lethal black claws.

I towered over Gregory, who stared at me in disbelief, "Look at you..." he breathed, "beautiful. And a thousand times bigger than this pup Taj."

Don't you dare speak of him that way. I released a threatening snarl. The growl did not stop him from understanding what I said. He knew nothing about my kind and was nothing but more than a puppet on a fucking string.

"What? You don't like how I talk about your wolf?" Gregory gave me a sideways smile. "What does it matter? He's *gone.*"

Instinct got the better of me as I launched myself at him. Gregory gave out a surprised grunt as he was thrown into the dirt. It was as if he overestimated my control or underestimated my fucking anger.

My claws dug into the Necromancer's chest. His face contorted in pain as he grabbed my furred wrists, desperately trying to pry them off, but my strength was unbearable.

"I didn't want to have to do this so early, but you leave me no choice," Gregory snarled. His eyes were glued to me as he uttered words in a foreign language, loud and clear. I recognized it as a spell only used in the darkest of magic. It was a Necromancer's call. A call to the spirits he's trapped and tortured to do his *Will.*

Thunder cracked in the distance; my heart dropped when I sniffed a familiar scent. I raised my head to see Taj creeping out from the shadows, a mile or so from us, in his complete wolf form.

What have you done to him?

I raised Gregory from the ground and slammed him into the nearest tree. The wood splintered.

The wolf... Taj bared his destructive canines. Not Taj... but an extension of the Necromancer because Taj was gone in the flesh. I had to set him free from this mess and let him move on as he should. He belonged with Kannuck, not stuck living in this existence, unable to watch over his child or be with his Mate in death.

The Necromancer's eyes glowed with magic. He barked another foreign order. Without a moment's hesitation, Taj leaped for me, knocking me off his master, his claws ripping through my skin as he pinned me to the ground. My chest stung from the long deep scratches, but I would take it, because I was not there to stop his soul from being taken.

I saw Gregory stand up, brushing the dirt off his clothes as if nothing had happened. Even as blood poured down his shirt, he strode toward us. That sick, demented smile plastered to his face again.

"I sense you have no desire to give me what I want," Gregory picked the dirt from his fingernails. "Which means I have no desire to give up what is rightfully mine."

Taj's soul is not *rightfully yours.* "He is my wolf and belongs to our God and me as his True Alpha!"

"If you give up now, I will cease my wolf's attack. You can go home to your Pack, and I can continue with my plan. We will never speak of this again."

He was fucking tripping if he thought that shit would fly.

I grabbed Taj's shoulders and heaved him off. The wolf came charging right back at me. I kicked into its muzzle, hard enough to send him flying, hoping it didn't hurt the real Taj behind the fur.

Taj whimpered at the kick and guilt-nagged at me, but I knew it would be temporary. I turned to pounce on Gregory again, but Taj intercepted me, biting hard into my shoulder.

I growled in pain and pushed him off. But Taj was relentless. As this twisted version of Taj attacked, Gregory's constant orders were all I could hear. No matter how many times he was pushed off. Again. And again. And again. He came back like a rabid animal, his jaws wide open and foam flowing through his teeth.

"That's enough! Enough!" I roared. I pinned Taj with an Alpha glare, and I knew the red ring in my eyes flared brightly. I pushed my command through my words, freezing the wolf in its place. The bites and scratches on my shoulders and torso bled into Taj's fur.

That was when I saw it. In Taj's eyes, a plea. As if to say...

I'm sorry. Taj was still there, his soul attached to a dead body. He was stuck here in pain and made to do things he would never have done to his Alpha.

It was only for a moment before he turned into a rabid animal once more.

Something within me shifted. My head turned to Gregory, who was chanting the Necromancer words to control Taj's body. His words mixed together with spells as he merged his Warlock powers with the dark energy of death magic. He pulled out a blade and slashed it across his chest. Gregory's chest began to bleed as blood dripped onto his shoes and the ground.

He would call more of his undead here. It was time to end this.

I sent an apology through my eyes, hoping Taj would forgive me for what I would do next and snapped the wolf's neck. The painful sound of his yelp echoed through the trees;

his body laid limp on the ground. I pulled in the fire and magic that now lived in my blood and body and shot out a powerful blast of fire. The orange and purple flames covered Taj's body, engulfing it in just seconds. I repeated words LaToya taught me about the power of fire and cleansing. It was all about intent and what was right.

Gregory cried out. I assumed it would take a few minutes for Gregory to reanimate his body. I didn't know. But it was enough time for me to submit myself entirely to my wolf form. I felt my body change, the burning rage taking over, and the instinct to kill. My eyes locked on Gregory, who paused his panicked chants and backed away, scampering up and disappearing through the trees. He could run, but he wouldn't be able to outrun me.

My hind legs pushed me into a run as I gave chase. Everything was clear, and my senses were sharper than ever. The red markings glowed as the fire fed my blood more and more energy.

My sight, smell, speed, and strength all heightened. All focused on the man who thought he could touch my Pack.

Kill. Said a quiet voice in my mind. That was the wild part of me, the part of me that is the True Alpha, who would do anything to protect its family and Pack. I let go and let it take control to do what it did best.

Kill, kill, kill.

It didn't take long to reach him in this form. I opened my mouth and breathed fire. It streamed from my mouth at the marked target. Gregory screamed as the fire reached him, consuming his flesh. I leaped as I growled viciously and stood over the top of Gregory's burning body.

Gregory gaped at me as fear flashed in his eyes because he knew what was up. This type of spell and fire burned to cleanse the flesh and the soul as well. In the distance, I heard Taj's howl and the pounding of paws rushing toward them.

But it was too late. I clamped my jaws down, letting my teeth sink into Gregory's fleshy throat. The fire did nothing to me because it was of me. The iron taste of blood poured onto my tongue, and I spoke the words to release the soul that belonged to me.

The rushing paw steps came to a halt. The Necromancer laid lifeless, expressionless, as the fire turned Gregory's body into ash. I turned and walked toward Taj's body. It was now unmoving. I looked at the husk, wishing there was another way to resolve things without killing, and let out a pained howl, hearing thunder cracking in the distance. I raised my clawed hand just as the red markings covered each finger and claw. I stabbed down into the chest of the wolf's body, pulling free a greenish-black heart. I raised it to the sky as I called on Kannuck to take his child home at last and let the magic of the spell incinerate the heart.

Goodbye. Be at peace. I could hear the scream, but it wasn't of pain this time. It was happiness for finally being free. I knew this had to be done, just as I knew this was not the end. Something was coming at us, and that shit was personal. It wanted to tear everything we were trying to build a part, but that shit was not about to happen. There are many of us, and if we all take on the responsibility of getting rid of the evil attacking us, we will end this crazy shit. I dropped to my knees and rested my forehead on the wolf, feeling the spirit leaving its body. *Rest.*

He was free now. The only thing that I had to do now was find the real Tucker and his son. I had wolves missing, which would not go down as long as I am the True Alpha.

Thunder cracked again–closer this time–as if in answer. And it began to rain. Everything happened at the time it was supposed to happen. I just prayed we could live up to the challenge set for us all.

~

Deadly Secrets

I STOOD up and ran toward the loud noises and explosions I could now make out. I shifted back into my human form just as I came to a cliff. I looked down and saw something holding my son. Then I saw Shani with Reign attached to her front. Then she shouted. "Riaan! Light them up!" I heard the scream and giggle as Riaan's entire body blazed to life. He was covered in fire, burning the thing that held onto him. It dropped my baby to the ground and I roared. I leaped down, but I saw Shani change before reaching the bottom. It wasn't in a wolf shifter way but something altogether different. Her body seemed to become a black hole. I knew she was there, but I couldn't see her or Reign. I landed on the sand in a crouch just as Shani reappeared in front of the large ***Akhkhazus.*** The Witch that controlled it stood there with wide eyes. Shani pulled her clawed hand back from her chest, pulling out her heart smoothly. Her clawed hands were tipped with gold as she squeezed the heart until it burst.

"Yucky Sha-Sha," Reign frowned. Her words seemed to catch Shani's attention as she shook herself. I cocked my head to the side as she blinked, seeming to regain control over her movements and thoughts. I moved over to Riaan, who was still laughing as the ***Akhkhazus*** burned. The body of the giant ass Cicada dropped once its master was dead.

"Enough, Riaan," I said, leaning over to pick him up.

"Da-da, fire. I fire," Riaan said as he rested his head on my shoulder. I looked at Shani as she stared blankly at her hand before noticing I was watching her.

"I...I don't know what this is, Quinn. What kind of power is this?"

I smiled because I knew she was far more than just a

normal wolf and more than a Delta. Before telling my little shadow it was all good, I saw a big ass bird in the sky and realized it was Damon.

"You got to be kidding me. Ain't no way, bro," I said. Shani turned around and looked up as Damon dropped down, and his large wings began to fade away.

"Are we done here, or y'all still playing around with burnt bugs and shit?"

"Where is LaToya?"

"Handling her business. Let's get back up there and help Blossom with the rest of this mess," Damon said. He turned as the wings we saw grew out of his back once more before he leaped into the air, leaving us to find our own way up.

"Is...I thought...he can't be an Angel, can he?" Shani asked. I honestly had no fucking idea.

"If he is, then there is more to that fool than anyone wants to admit. But the things he has done don't seem too far from the truth."

I wanted to know where Damon "Demon" Vaughn got Angel wings. That shit should not even be possible, but he was flying around like he was the shit. I shook my head, trying to concentrate. I knew he had my back out there, so I shouldn't have to worry about anything coming up behind me. I pushed forward, ready to get this shit down and make Ellen punk-ass pay for what she has done.

The fire roared through my veins like an unstoppable heat of rage I couldn't quench. My hands balled into fists as I gripped my gun tightly. On the other hand, my nails dug into my skin, drawing blood.

"Ellen!" I spat the name as a burst of flames erupted from my fingertips. I stepped inside the structure where I became the head of my Circle, but things were different. Once my foot stepped inside, it was like I had traveled through a portal. I stepped into an open clearing in the forest. The trees had been scorched to nothing, and the ground was blackened as if this place held no life. It was nothing like the beautiful land we had just left behind. No one else would be as destructive with their magic. That was how I knew Ellen was here. "Reveal yourself!"

I felt the heat of a fire that wasn't my own before it

appeared before me. The dead leaves on the forest floor lit up as an infernal wall ignited around me, disappearing mere seconds after it surfaced. It left a rich, heavy smoke trail directly to the person I came here to kill.

Ellen, clothed in black, emerged from the smoke like a Goddess she wished she could be. The Witch was armed to the teeth with blades while her markings covered her right arm to her neckline.

"I don't believe that's any way to speak to your aunt, LaToya," she smiled thinly. I ground my teeth together, shooting Ellen a deadly glare.

"Don't play with me," I snarled, "give me the boy. Where the hell is Zaccai?"

"You are in no position to be making demands." Ellen chuckled. I gripped the gun tighter, trying to reserve my shots. I was nowhere near filled up in power, but I could feel the glove trying to pull in the magic surrounding us. I just needed more time.

I didn't have time for her shit, so I refused to wait. I bared my teeth at her, ensuring she knew my following words were a threat. "Where the fuck is Zaccai?"

Ellen sighed. The bitch had the nerve to sigh as if I was asking for a favor. She took something from me not once but twice now, and I was about done with the bullshit! Ellen turned her head, looking to the deep thicket of trees behind her, and called out to Zaccai. "Sweetheart? Make yourself known, dear."

My eyes snapped to where Ellen gazed, heart racing in anticipation. A small, withered voice called out from the trees.

"Toya?" My heart hitched and a chill spread through my spine.

"Zaccai."

I couldn't see anything clearly through the night sky, but I had no hesitation running for the voice as I called out his name. "Zaccai! Answer me, baby!"

Ellen was quick. My arm screamed in pain when a burning hand gripped me, jerking me to a halt.

"I think not, little niece."

"Get the hell off me!" I growled.

I couldn't move as Ellen whirled around, trapping me with an arm hooked around my neck. I felt a hidden blade pressed hard against my back, widening my eyes. I had to get it together because I trained for shit like this. Marcus drilled Taria and me relentlessly until we could fight without magic or weapons. I had to get out of my own way, but how? How when Zaccai was alone and afraid? The blade pressed harder, but it was not enough to hurt. It was enough to cut through the fabric and nip my skin.

My racing thoughts and beating heart stilled like the dead —silent like a grave.

"You don't want to do this, Ellen," I breathed, "I don't want to hurt you."

Ellen chuckled, "that's cute." She leaned closer, the blade pressing harder as her lips touched the shell of my ear. "*You* don't want to hurt *me*?"

I let out a hiss through gritted teeth as the smell of burning skin hit me. The fire Witch had sent heat through the blade, searing dangerously close to my spine. "I wonder what your mother would think if she saw you now," Ellen jeered. "Just a pathetic Witchling. One who is not meant to hold the Grey power."

The mention of my mother, who was lost to me forever, stunned the pain and panic right out of me. And now Ellen had Zaccai in her clutches. I would be found dead before I let Ellen take another from me. The whispers came strong, crashing into my mind as my hand began to heat up. I remembered the gun and the spelled rounds it held.

A tether that held something deep inside me snapped. A wave of anger shot through me and a rush of power I hadn't felt before. It felt old, but as if it had always been a part of me. The jolt went through my body, screaming as a spark ignited within me. I felt a wave of power and strength unleash into a wave of flames that spread through the open clearing of the forest. I twisted away and spun around, then aimed. My vision focused on Ellen, who leaped backward, but it was like my vision had sharpened. I remember it happened once with Quinn, and that's when I felt the power. My markings covered every inch of my body, and a red haze bled over my eyes. I could see everything down in detail. I pulled the trigger as I released a blast of fire, shocking Ellen. She barely managed to miss the bullets, but she couldn't outrun that fire. I was already moving, feeling like I was running on four legs instead of two. I was on that bitch before her next blink. I lifted a heel while spinning in place and jabbed it backward into Ellen's shin, followed by a brutal headbutt into her nose.

Ellen let out a grunt as she staggered back, a small falter but enough for me to shift my position to kick her in the stomach, sending her flying back. It created distance between us, giving me a chance to deal with the voices screaming in my mind.

"Don't you *ever* speak of her," I cried, "*you* have no right!"

Ellen reached for her nose, a drop of blood smearing on her fingers. She smiled, "You truly have a death wish, don't you?" A burst of flames lit and rested upon Ellen's hand, a mix of blue, red, and gold dancing and weaving around her bloodied fingers. Ellen began to circle me. "If you back down now, perhaps I will spare Zaccai the same fate your mother met. His soul would do well to serve my Goddess."

I narrowed my eyes because I wanted to know who was behind her in all of this. Where was she getting this amount of power from? I knew it wasn't natural. I could see the dark tendrils of evil laced through her fire, and it was strong as hell. A wave of fiery anger rose in my chest at how Ellen could betray the Witchy world and her own family for fucking power. A power that did not belong to her! It was clear what Ellen was trying to do, but if I risked another explosion, I was afraid my magic would burn out. The glove was working and pulling on my enteral magic, but I couldn't let my emotions get the best of me. I couldn't let the whispers of death, despair, and sorrow get further into my head. If I let go again, I would barely have an ember left. I knew the power of Twice Marked was pumping through me, but I did not want to draw more on it because I knew my Mate would need every bit of it when he found Gregory. The voice screamed for me to die and just give in and join the rest of my dead siblings. I frowned because I was an only child. Then a rage burned through me as I realized what the other voices were screaming.

Fight for us: Sister, our blood.

Fight for us. Save us. She has us!

That's when it all made sense, and I thought back to the day I gave birth. I knew the smokey evil in my dreams was Ellen. What I didn't notice was what was attached to her energy. Yes, she wanted to kill me, but she wanted my children more. That's when Baron's words came back to me. *I will not let Brijit take you or my grandchildren from me.* She wanted to end my bloodline, just as she had done before. So she is using my own family against me. That fucking bitch! I took a deep breath before I lost my mind. She knew about me, and her plans were already in motion from the beginning!

Don't blow up... Not yet.

I inhaled, summoning the flame, a calm, quiet flame dancing through my veins, and a flashing flame came up on my hand. The other voices were my brothers and sisters who she had already taken from this world, and I would be damned if I was next!

I hear you! I hear you all!

"Back down?" I growled. "And let you take one of my own? Do you think you can take me down for some trumped-up fake ass Goddess who man didn't want that old coochie anymore? Fuck you and that death-eating bitch!" I sent a chilling glare while understanding what Damon had been saying as it dawned on me.

Ellen smirked, "I will kill you for that, feed your soul and that boy to my Goddess, just like I did your mother! Very well, LaToya Aja Grey." Then a ball of flames headed in my direction. I was quick to block it with my own, rolling away from the ball's target. I poised myself for a physical attack, bending my knees, so I was stable. Calm as water. Light as air. I let the elements fill me and speak to me openly while opening my mind to all the voices who tried bending me to their *Will.* I didn't know what she thought she knew about me, but Ellen knew absolutely nothing if she thought all I had was fire up my sleeve.

Ellen had experience with her element making her quick, wise, and precise. And she knew how to salvage it. What she didn't have was a familiar. She was alone, thinking that giving up her own personal power would bring her something greater. Our familiars weren't a tool but a part of our magic to make it more extraordinary. Nuriel never once told me how to use my fire, never did more than what I knew because I hadn't embraced all of me. All of my gifts, magic, and bloodline. They say death magic is evil and dark, but the hottest fire can cleanse if you accept it and use it correctly. That is what I am and what I can do. I can cleanse this evil and save those who have been tainted by death if I just kill the one who started down this path. *Brijit* would die and I would set my siblings free.

Ellen didn't pause, running toward me, the glint of a knife shone in my eyes, and I was quick to dodge, but only the blur of wild red and gold was in sight before the sharp end of a blade sliced the side of my waist.

I cursed, biting my tongue.

I felt my powers growing, and I could feel Nuriel approaching as if I called out to him. I needed something to slow Ellen down.

Ellen let out a dark laugh as she created a ring of fire around us. I kept a tight lid on my powers, making her believe I was weak. I kept my stance, but it wasn't enough. I was sent back into the firewall, when Ellen threw a brutal punch that was followed by another summoned flame, burning off a large portion of my shirt. I howled in pain as I dropped the empty gun, raising my hand to hold my blistered skin. I had to hold out for just a little bit longer as I broke down the walls and roadblocks in my mind. I knew my mother thought she was protecting me when she put the spell over me, but all it did was block my true power. It only blocked my birth-given power from my father's blood.

The heatwaves were blinding. Rolls of sweat covered my forehead like beads.

Ellen was practically invisible in this heat. She moved swiftly and threw punches with deadly accuracy on every spot of my body that would cause the most pain. I was skilled enough to dodge most of them, but even I could feel the warmth of the blood as a large gash opened from another knife attack.

I needed to tame the ring of fire. But how...

An idea struck me.

It was risky. It was so incredibly risky that I knew it had to be done. Damon once said that if you are not cheating, you're not winning. This spell could collapse everything around us and destroy this plane if I did it wrong. I lowered myself, placing my fingertips on the earth, summoning the forest's moisture from the ground. Droplets emerged from the dead soil, grouping themselves together, extinguishing the fire as it turned to steam.

My head was spinning because I didn't know how much blood I'd lost and it was getting harder to see, but I stayed focused. I pulled on the wolf, and it sharpened my vision, giving me a boost of healing energy. I used the water element to rid the fire area, clearing a path to that bitch.

A blur of black flashed before me, and I smiled, *found you.*

Ellen charged forward, attacking from the front. Swift as lightning, I pinned her down, meeting her gaze with a raging ferocity I had never released before. I could've sworn I saw a flash of fear in the fire Witch's eyes when she saw my expression. I felt Nuriel then, and his power entered my body, giving me life again as my powers fully returned. My tank was full, and I felt heat like I had never had before. It was hotter than my own and burned hotter than the fires of Hell.

"I would be lying if I said I don't want to hurt you, Ellen," I gritted. Ellen tried to wriggle out of my grip, but I began to grow. I felt this little portal shake as I stood, and I began to see the tops of trees as cracks in the dark sky began to form.

"I am here, little Witch. Your mind is open and clear. Can't you feel the magic that burns in our blood?"

Nuriel's voice soothed something inside of me as the world Ellen created broke around us. I stood where I once was before stepping into the building.

"Yes, I feel it. It's volatile, like a volcano."

"Yes, now you must start your training with the fire elemental. Katara has been waiting for you and Taria. It is time. This is a form you will be able to take, but this is just a teaser for now. You are not ready for the full extent."

I looked around and saw Damon's slack-jawed expression at my height. I finally was taller than everyone, and I felt I could pluck his wings right out of the sky. I had to give it to him because he wasn't so bad. His words opened my mind to see what I didn't want to see. I didn't want something to make me evil, but something couldn't just turn you evil unless you gave into it. Damon made a choice, but he never gave in to the darkness even when it tortured him, so neither would I.

I looked down at my aunt, who smiled widely — psychotically — spitting a mouthful of blood over her face. "You are as much a fool as your mother was. It's funny how that ended her, and now it is what will end you. This magic is too much for you and that weak bloodline! Your father was no one, just a human who meant nothing!" Ellen's hand pried free and reached for a blade before I could act quick enough.

The crude black blade would have cut into me had I not thrown Ellen to the side in time. I could feel the soul-sucking magic coming from the blade, and I knew I had to keep that thing away from me. I took a giant step forward as Ellen used her fire to cover her body and rise into the air. I wanted to know more about this form and how to use it. Nuriel was just showing off, but I could feel his eminent power and raw energy as if it were my own.

How dare this bitch speak about my mother that way? How *dare* she?

I gathered every flicker of energy from within and summoned a firestorm, unleashing that ferocity again. I used the screams in my head as an assault directed at Ellen, making her cry out in pain. The souls and lives she has taken raged at her once they knew who to blame.

The heat of the fire cracked in my veins, ruthless, merciless. I reveled in the terror that flashed in Ellen's eyes when the flame was released. Terror of such untamed *raw* power. I used my air element to feed the flame, making it hotter. I could see it changing colors, from blue, white, green, orange, and purple.

Ellen tried to back away. She truly backed away as if she didn't deserve worse than death like this.

"I will give you one chance, *aunt,* since you have shown

such disinterest in being civil with me." I rumbled as powerful and loud as my flames. "I can force the fate you chose for my mother upon you...or... you *run*. Run back to that bitch and tell her I am coming. I will not stop until all of you are ground under my heels!"

Ellen didn't need to be told twice. She fell from the sky and fell into a panicked sprint toward the darkness like a true coward. I felt her speaking a language and using a spell to connect to that hoe ass Brijit. That was all I needed her to do. "Thanks for that knowledge, but I changed my mind." I roared and let the fire I saved up shoot out toward Ellen. She must have felt the heat coming as she tried and failed to make a portal. I held all the gates closed and locked this bitch down tightly. The different color fires mixed and swirled together, making me think about Kon's eyes as they crashed into her like a tidal wave.

"AHHH! No! NO! Goddess! Goddess, save me!" Ellen screamed while I watched the fire consume her body and evil black soul. I watched her disappear with the satisfaction of avenging my mother's death. I knew that Ellen wasn't as powerful as she let on, and it had come from Brijit. I knew my true enemy, and I was gunning for that bitch.

"Child! Do you think that little display of power means anything to a Being such as I? Your power means nothing to me, and I will own your soul the same way I own your mother's!"

The voice sounded like smooth steel over velvet, but the shrieking and shouts were what held my attention. That voice scream was Rhonda! That voice was my mother!

As soon as the heavy power vanished, so did my flames and height. I collapsed onto the dirt, coughing blood into my palms. I felt the calling of sleep pulling me away. I felt as if I had used every ounce of my magic and that last act drained the hell out of me.

Zaccai. I had to get up for him.

I dragged myself toward the nearest tree, using it to pick myself up off the ground. "Zaccai!" I called out, cringing at the pain it caused for me to speak. The building was now in ruins and crumbling to the ground like paper. I looked past the tree line and saw a glint of metal shining in the distance. Was that a cage? I moved, and I felt the rush of fire run through my blood once more as the whispers hummed in contentment in the back of my mind. I squinted at the cylindrical shape hanging from a low branch of a tree.

"Toya?"

I saw a faint movement from the cage and rushed towards it.

There he was, chained and blindfolded. If the two wet patches where his eyes were didn't tell me he had been crying, then the faint silver streaking his cheeks certainly did. I should have chopped off Ellen's head for this alone.

"Oh, god, Zaccai!" I exhaled in relief. Zaccai's chains rattled as he rushed to the side of the cage, where he heard my voice.

I grabbed the cage lock and burned through the metal, along with his chains. He threw himself into my arms and I clutched him tight. I could tell he tore the blindfold off before I saw it floating to the ground.

I hissed in pain, and he loosened his grip to look me over.

"Oh no... I'm so sorry," he uttered softly, staring at my injuries. "Is my mom here? I have to tell her I'm sorry," he said.

I fell to my knees and looked down; my gash had been far deeper than I thought. I winced, seeing the white of my bone peeking through the blood. I must have been hit harder than I thought to be feeling this pain now.

"Come on, help me up," I ordered. Zaccai did not hesitate in holding my hand as we stood. "Your mom isn't here, but we will get you to her soon. She is so worried, and I am sure you have nothing to be sorry for," I said, gasping in pain. I released the power of the Twice Marked a minute ago, so I knew healing was about to get real as shit.

"Are you going to be okay?" He asked.

I grinned at his pure face contorted with concern, "Of course I will," I said, looking around for any sight of other Witches or Warlocks. He smiled at me and held out his hands, which glowed a warm yellow. He placed his tiny hands over my wounds, and the energy felt like sunshine and smelled like honeysuckles. "Oh wow, that's nice," I smiled. Zaccai looked up and smiled again.

"It's just a little something, but it might make you sleepy," he said. I opened my mouth, then felt myself falling face-first into the dirt. Hot, large, and strong arms surrounded me as Nuriel caught me. Everything went peacefully blank.

CHAPTER 20 DAMON

This entire situation was wild, and I never thought I would see the shortest person I knew grow enough not to need a booster seat to drive. That Fire Giant gave her a leg up in the height department, if only for a few moments. After dropping Zaccai off with the Rayne Pack, we headed back to the school, and for some reason, I couldn't wait. I needed some time alone after all this bullshit to put things in perspective.

"We are damn near home y'all! Don't tell anyone about this RV getting messed up, either. I put it back together, so no snitching," Toya yelled.

"Naw, don't any one of you talk about my wings. Forget the RV! We are the only ones who need to know about that shit," I growled. I said it more for Toya than anyone because she liked to run off at the mouth about shit.

"Boy, if you believe I would tell anyone how closely you resemble an actual Angel, you're trippin! Naw, no one needs to know," Toya shook her head. At least her short ass agreed with me because I wasn't really worried about anyone else. Shani seemed to be in her own head, and Quinn could not care less. He probably would run his mouth to Michael, but I think he had a lot more on his mind than worrying about me. I had to respect the dog for being able to take down that bitch, Gregory. Gregory deserved the punishment Quinn put down on his ass. But knowing there were more out here pissed me the fuck off. More souls were being stolen before they could pass on as they should. I may not know anything about Jessiah and his *Kindred,* but they were still family when Necromancers attacked them as well. The fact that a Necromancer held him that long and I couldn't do anything to help him still had me biting my tongue when Ash came around. He knew this entire time what had happened, but said nothing. I was offered a chance to save one brother but leave the other to a fate no one should endure. It was bullshit, just like I still had to find the other half of my soul, but I didn't know what demon held it. I knew Apu had something to do with it, but I didn't think he had it, and that bastard Ashriel wouldn't tell me. Fuck it. I will figure it out on my own. I felt eyes on me, and when I turned, I saw Blossom watching me from the shadows. She sat across from me, leaning back into the couch, pulling in the surrounding darkness. The only thing I could see was her swirling eyes.

"Do you agree, Blossom?"

"If my Queen asks me if you have wings, I will tell her the truth. If no one asks, I don't see the need to bring up something so inconsequential. They are just wings," she stated. I heard her words, but I could feel the hidden curiosity she tried to hide. She wanted to know about them, which just made a slow smile cross my face.

"Aight, that is not a problem. They are just wings and are nothing special."

Blossom narrowed her eyes at me but said nothing. I knew what she was thinking and what everyone else would be thinking if they weren't caught up in their own shit. How in the hell would a Vampire have the wings of an Angel? Blossom was damn sure older than I was, and she has seen things I am sure that haven't crossed my path, so the question on her mind would be, am I one of these so-called Fallen? The things I have done and the demons using me would make it seem that way, and it's honestly what I thought. Now that I have my memories back, I remember the day I was born. I remember when the world cried for us all. I heard animals fleeing and the storms raging. I knew others probably believed it was because of the evil inside me because I did as well. But I know different now. Who could it be if it wasn't me the world cried for? Something else happened on that day, and we needed to find out what. If we want to get ahead of this shit, we have to start digging deeper into the past. It was about time we actually questioned our grandmother about what we were really meant to be doing and who is our grandfather exactly. What is he, and where is he now? The RV jerked to the side, breaking my thoughts.

"Damn, Toya, ease up on the gas. How the hell are you speeding for someone who can barely reach the pedals?" I grunted. As heat and fire rushed through my veins, my head snapped to the window. Blossom was already up, her eyes bleeding to crimson as she stared out the window at the sky. I hadn't had a feeling like this before, but the sudden recognition in my blood made little sense.

"Something is out there!" Blossom growled. I didn't know why her hackles were up, but I would take her lead until we knew what the fuck was happening.

"Did anybody see that big ass snake in the fucking air? I know I am not going crazy!" Toya shrieked. Quinn was looking out of the front window, but I could tell he couldn't see anything either, but I could feel something. It felt almost similar to Selena, but more.

"Slow down. Let's not let it onto the property until we know who and what it is," Quinn stated.

"Unc D! Unc D, look," Riaan screamed. I turned around to

see him flamed out and breathing fire. Shani had her head in her hands, shaking her head, as Reign laughed.

"Ri-Ri like dis," Reign laughed as she growled.

"What the fuck have you been teaching the children, Blossom?"

"Oh no, don't you blame this on me! I don't know what this is," Blossom stated. I saw the flicker of a smile, but her intense glare never left the sky. I looked back out the window as we slowed down twenty feet from the school's gate. Quinn passed by me to get his crazy-ass kids in line as I stood to see what the hell was coming.

"Reign and Riaan, be quiet now. Listen to Shani and stay in your chairs," Quinn demanded. The giggling and growling became quiet, but I didn't wait for anyone else. I opened the door and stepped outside with Toya right behind me.

"Is Nuriel still with you?"

"You think we need the big gun for this?"

"I think we will need a massive gun or a fucking rocket."

"Why? What–,"

"Look up," I said. Honestly, I could not believe what I saw because I had never seen one other than Selena. But this Dragon was way more massive than our grandmother, and the wingspan was larger than anything I had ever heard about or read.

"Holy fucking shit! Wait...wait, is someone riding that thing? Somebody is on top of it!" Toya screamed as the wings beat a gust of wind in our direction. The Dragon's gold seemed to shine brighter than Michael's eyes, but the glow of fire in its eyes told of ancient intelligence.

"Ahh, I...I think that's Lydia," Quinn said, standing next to us. The Dragon landed a reasonable distance from us, but the shift's speed was almost like magic. One minute it was as large as a cruise ship, and the next, a tall man with eyes of flames holding a petite woman in his arms stood in the grass.

"I think that is...he is..." I didn't know what exactly to say and that had never happened to me before. The closer the two came toward us, the more features I could make out. I felt like I was about to stumble or run because the man looked like he could have been my father, except for one difference. His eyes weren't gold, and a Dragon's tattoo would not have been on his chest.

"Toya, Quinn, is that you? Wait, Damon, hold up, I thought...wait a minute," Lydia stuttered. She looked confused, but I became concerned when I focused on her more. If I hadn't had Taria's blood lingering in my body, I might not have seen the chains of shadows wrapped around her body like a bruise.

"I am a long story, Lydia, but you have a better story. Why are you *Condemned*?" I asked. I heard Toya suck in a breath as she let the fire covering her arms dye away, and the beast in Quinn's eyes faded as we realized they were not here to hurt us.

"She is this way because of me. I did this to her," the Draakian said. He pulled Lydia closer to him, but his eyes never left mine. His head cocked to the side as he studied me, almost making me ask him if he had a problem, but I knew power. He was an old, old power that hadn't been born but was created by the creator.

"Sire, stop! I did this of my own free *Will*, and I would do it again. Either way, we do not have time for all this. I need to speak with Michael about what has happened and about Derrick. He needs to know of the imminent threat and...and that Derrick is dead. My parents killed him and imprisoned me," Lydia exhaled sharply.

"Wait! Wait a minute. Derrick isn't dead," Toya said, taking a step forward. We felt a crushing power, but it didn't bother me. I knew who it was just as I figured out who this Dragon was to me. Sire Daemon is my Uncle and the ruler of Draakian kind. We looked to the sky as a roar of something just as significant as Sire came barreling toward the ground. With a flash of golden light, my grandmother Selena stood with eyes of fire in front of her brother.

"Sire?"

"Selena? Selena, where...how is..."

I felt a warm hand grip mine as a familiar scent of sweet strawberries, and home filled the surrounding air. I looked down and saw Taria standing there and Michael next to her with the exact same look I had as the brother and sister greeted each other.

"Michael!" Lydia screamed, and he moved. She stood in front of him with her head down, like Michael was about to take her head. I looked at Toya, who studied the Dragons in fascination, and I knew it was because their fire called to hers. I knew I would have to let her know she might just have a Dragon in her lineage somewhere in the Grey bloodline, but that was another story.

"Lydia! Derrick is on the way home. We thought... he went back for you, but no one was there," Michael stated.

"What? Wait, he made it. He told you what happened?"

"Yes, but that can wait. You are home now. That is all that matters. It has been months," Michael said.

"Months? That can't be right, maybe weeks, but not months."

"Naw, he is right, Lydia. It has been a good minute, but that isn't important right now. I want to know about these chains," Taria said. Lydia looked at her with hope in her eyes as she hugged Taria.

"Short story is, Sire was chained in a cavern where I was taken. I used what magic I knew to help, but it required that I take on his burden. He is my *Kindred*, so I did what I had to do," Lydia said. I caught Sire's gaze as he pulled away from Selena and moved to stand with Lydia.

"You all may not know me, but you do know Lydia, and I

beg that you help her," Sire asked. Michael looked at me and then at Selena, who had tears of flames rolling down her cheeks.

"Sire, you are my family. You do not need to ask for anything. We have some catching up to do, but I know my wife will help Lydia. We will find the demon that holds her soul," Michael stated. Taria let go of my hand, then touched Lydia like she was trying to see what had a hold of her when I felt her at my back. I knew Blossom was there without me having to turn around. Her eyes still held that crimson glow, but the tension was no longer in her body. Her arm brushed mine as her fingertips lingered on mine for just a second. It was almost like she needed the contact.

"My Queen, I..." Taria spun around and gave Blossom a raised eyebrow. "Sorry, Taria. I think I may know the demon who holds the claim of her soul."

"What! Who is it so I can kill them?" Taria said as lightning flashed in the distance. Blossom just smiled as if she liked when the crazy-ass Vampire Hunter Queen got bloodthirsty. I mean, I did too because it was fun. It reminded me of our Hell days when it was all killing and running.

"I don't think you would want to kill your Shade, but I offer my life for hers if you want them," Blossom stated.

"Whoa, hold the fuck up!" I shouted.

"Damon, shut up. No one is killing your obsession," Toya laughed as she brushed me aside. "There is always another way, right?" She asked Taria and Blossom. Taria and Blossom stared at one another, communicating silently as everyone waited for the answer. Taria smiled and then looked at me before laughing.

"Okay, so Damon, remember the race you tried to cheat on, and we left Blossom?"

"Yes, and I was teaching you a valuable lesson in the art of winning," I defended. Michael glared at me, but I waved his ass off.

"Well, apparently Blossom may have killed a legion of demons, and one of them happens to be a Soul Collector," Taria said.

"Yes, it was one, and now I hold the souls that it has collected. I felt the change when you two must have traded places. At the time, I did not know what happened or who it belonged, but it wasn't necessary to search for anything. I have your soul Lydia Parks, and I release you from the bonds of the shadows and freely return to you what should have never been taken." Blossom whispered. We all felt the sudden rush of power surround us, then slam violently into Lydia, making her gasp, but no scream came out of her mouth. Sire held her body to his as the shadow chains each became visible to the eyes, then the smokey darkness flaked away as if they never existed.

I looked at Blossom, seeing the swirling colors return to her eyes as she stepped back. She looked at me, then stepped backward, disappearing into the shadows as if she owned them all. Something was up, and I was going to find out what it was and what that Shade was hiding from me.

"They're gone! Sire, it's done." Lydia cried. I took a step back and watched each of them, wondering what part will they play in this war that was coming. I witnessed LaToya's breakthrough, grow into her power, and accept who she is and what she can do. I saw Quinn destroy a Warlock using magic that he should not be capable of doing. I knew what I did for my brother was the right thing to do, but I was not sure that sticking around to be the guide was the right choice until this moment. My problem is that it wasn't only my family that needed me. There is another, and I was going to break those walls. Blossom thinks she can put between us. I just might need a little more of the pixie dust shit to get it done.

"Oh my God, Taria! Damon has Wings! I mean real wings! Baby duck feathers and all!"

My head snapped around to see the short Witch standing in heels and let my fangs grow to my chin.

"I knew I should have drained your ass instead of Taria that day!"

"See, I told y'all he is a DEMON!" She screamed and ran. I knew those short stubby legs wouldn't make it far, but that thing in my chest moved slightly. I could feel she was not truly afraid of me anymore, making me feel like the grinch when his heart grew, and it was bullshit. I wouldn't say I liked emotions, but it wasn't all bad when I saw the twins smiling at me as they babbled a language I swear I had heard before. That was impossible, though, because it had died out before I was born, and I only heard it because my father knew the language.

"Come on, creatures, let's go play in mommy's new closet," I grinned as I picked them up and disappeared.

EPILOGUE
LATOYA

My mind still raced as I went through the motions of being a mother and wife. We had done what needed to be done, but I knew there were still other Witches and Warlocks that would not fall in line. I managed to kill the cancer that infected my family, but it didn't mean that the evil didn't spread. The Circles that followed *Brijit* would be found and put down with prejudice. I wished they were all in one spot, but that would have been too easy. Ellen may be dead, but what she started has opened a gateway for *Brijit* to manipulate my people. We still had to clean house in all of our families and get them in order, but something inside told me that it was best if we did it all together.

After I got the twins settled and kissed Kon until he ran away, I was able to shut myself into my meditation room. I wanted to talk to Taria about everything that had happened and began making plans to deal with the bastards that kept coming for us. I would, but first, I had to do one thing. I needed answers about *Brijit* that only one *Being* could give to me, and he seemed not to want to answer me. Fuck all that noise because if I had to punch a hole back into Hell, I would just to find that plane where his ass lived. I needed my father to actually be a father and tell me what I needed to know. I knew *Brijit* had a lot to do with what went down, and *Idh* played a hand in the bullshit as well. My question is, are they working together or naw? I wanted to know where my mother's soul was and if it was true that the bitch really was holding her hostage. I wanted to scream and beat something to death, but I knew I had to keep it together.

I closed the door and stood in the middle of a dark room that was surrounded by mirrors. My reflection stared back at me, no matter which way I turned. The whispers in my head were now a familiar hum of noise, but I knew that I was in charge. I knew they needed me to guide them to where they belonged, and the ones who didn't want to leave, it was my job to send them, anyway.

"I know you can hear me. I need you to answer me, Baron!" I turned in a circle, looking into each dark mirror as I continued to call his name. I clenched my fists tightly, trying to hold on to my temper, but fuck it.

"Baron! I swear if I have to punch another hole to where you are, I will do it! Tell me where my mother is and how I can get her back! Why is this happening?" I shook from the force of my emotions, and I knew Quinn would feel it. I tried sending calming energy his way, but that wouldn't stop him from coming to see what was up.

"We should not be talkin child."

"Fuck that! I want to know if you know that bitch has my mother's soul?" Everything went silent, and then I felt a cold presence as a face appeared in the mirror in front of me. I looked up into eyes that glowed with a power I couldn't comprehend.

"This can not be true. She would not dare. Your mother should still be watching over you."

"Oh, she dares because she is not. I don't know what kind of arrangement you had with your wife, but she has been trying to come to me since birth. I don't know if she is working with *Idh*, but I want you to tell her something. You tell her that I am coming for her ass, and no amount of allies, puppets, souls, or powers will fucking stop me."

"*Idh*? She is no friend of our kind, more of an enemy."

"Well, an enemy of an enemy is my friend, I guess, because they sure had to be working together. They may not be working toward the same goals, but they used one another."

"This is a line that even *Brijit* can not come back from, and her assault on you has sealed her fate. If she holds your mother's soul, I will find her."

"Not just me, Baron. She has killed any children you have ever had, and she has their souls. How could you not have known?" I felt the rage and anger as if the wind of a tornado had blasted me.

"That is impossible!"

"I could hear them! They want to be freed. She has them just as she has Rhonda! What are you going to do about it? No more sitting on the sidelines. It's time to pick which side you are on." I wanted to ask about these children and who they were and what kind of marriage arrangement these Gods and Goddess had, but I didn't care. I only knew that I had to set my mother free and save the souls who called out to me for help.

"I walked every one of my children to the other side. For her to defy their rightful peace is unforgivable. It is time for my house to enter this war. We will retrieve your mother's soul and end *Brijit* once and for all. I will walk the earth once more, LaToya Aja Grey, stand with my true family, and stand by my daughter's side."

I blinked and opened my mouth, but he was already gone. The mirror was empty of all but my own reflection. I knew there were more answers that I needed and things we were missing, but since things were quiet, it was about time we attacked first.

The End

AUTHOR'S NOTE

Thank you for reading. I hope you enjoy the series so far! Please review I love them or feel free to contact me on Facebook, Twitter, Instagram, good reads, book bub, or through my website. Thank you again for reading and keep looking for more Deadly Secrets series!

Follow or contact me at the links below to see what is coming up next!

www.ebowserbooks.com

www.facebook.com/authorE.Bowser

https://www.bookbub.com/authors/e-bowser

https://www.goodreads.com/ebowser

Twitter: @ebowser0110

IG:@e.bowserbooks

TikTok: @ebowserauthor

E. Bowser is an author of Paranormal Romance, Fantasy, and Horror. E. Bowser loves to come home and write whatever stories come to mind. E. Bowser always wanted to write a story that people would like to read and give their feedback to make her next better. She loves to read herself and takes great pleasure in doing so. In middle school, E. Bowser started writing short stories about life, anything horror or paranormal. E. Bowser loves to write whatever her imagination can come up with over a cup of tea.

BOOKS BY THE AUTHOR

Deadly Secrets Brothers That Bite Books 1-5

The Deadly Secrets is an exciting series focused on Taria, Michael Quinn and LaToya are friends and lovers fighting against evil forces.

Deadly Secrets Awakening Book 1

Deadly Secrets Revealed Book 2

Deadly Secrets Consequences Book 3

Deadly Secrets Consequences Book 4

Deadly Secrets Royalty Book 5

Deadly Secrets Novellas

This collection of stories will give you a glimpse into the lives of Taria, Michael, LaToya, and Quinn, along with many others. Sit back and fall back into the paranormal world of Deadly Secrets.

Desires of the Harvest Moon

Twice Marked Witches and Wolves

Rise of the Phoenix

A Vampire and His Alpha Mate

A Hunter Touched My Soul

Brothers That Bite Chronicles Volume 1

Trick or Treat: The Babysitters From Hell (Short)

Rescued By Fire: Gio & Selena (Novelette)

Scorched By Desire: Sire & Lydia's Story (Novelette)

The Crown Series Books 1-3 On-Going Series

This series would be best read if you start with Deadly Secrets Series Brothers That Bite books 1-5 and other novellas.

Taria, LaToya, Michael, and Quinn are back together again in Deadly Secrets Hunters Regin: The Crown Series. Taria Cross was turned into a Vampire by Michael Vaughn, and she became his Queen. Not only does she have to figure out this new part of her life, but she is a Hunter as well, and that is a whole other list of duties.

Deadly Secrets Hunters Reign Book 1

Deadly Secrets A Vampires Temptation Book 2

Their Sirenian Queen

Deadly Secrets When Queens Are Crowned Book 3

The Rayne Pack Series On-Going Series

Follow the Rayne Brothers as they find their Mates and fight the forces of evil. See how Dax, Max, Malic, Alex, Jarod, and Thomas fight for those they love while being attacked on all sides.

An Alpha's Claim Book 1

Dream Walker: Visions of the Dead On-Going Series.

What if you had the ability to see things before they happened? Saw a zombie outbreak unfold before your very eyes? Could you embrace visions of the dead coming back to life? For Kaylee, who has been chosen to receive this gift, these visions are the beginning of a nightmare.

Dream Walker: Visions of the Dead Book 1

Dream Walker: Visions of the Dead Book 2

Dream Walker: Visions of the Dead Book 3

Dream Walker The Unknown Stories Kindle Vella Stories

www.ingramcontent.com/pod-product-compliance
Lightning Source LLC
Chambersburg PA
CBHW081139300726
48982CB00006B/1011

* 9 7 9 8 9 8 5 5 5 2 5 4 6 *